RENEGADE BLOOD KILL

Over the confusion of battle, Rebecca heard angry sounds in an unfamiliar dialect and turned to see an Apache aim his rifle at her. She dropped from *Sila*'s saddle to the ground and started firing wildly.

The warrior's bullet cracked overhead and her horse ran out of the way. With a clearer field of fire, Rebecca pumped two bullets from her big Bisley into the Indian as he ran toward her.

He staggered, stopped and turned sideways, then fell face first in the blood-soaked soil on the battle-field.

#23

COMANCHE COME DOWN
E.J. HUNTER

ZEBRA BOOKS
KENSINGTON PUBLISHING CORP.

Special acknowledgements to Mark K. Roberts.

"Speculators and men wishing the presence of troops are greater enemies and need more watching than the Indians."

> —*Lt. Col. Orville E. Babcock,*
> *Inspecting Officer.*
> *House Ex. Docs., 39th Cong.,*
> *2d session, No. 20, p. 5.*

ZEBRA BOOKS

are published by

Kensington Publishing Corp.
475 Park Avenue South
New York, NY 10016

First printing: October, 1991

Printed in the United States of America

1

Sunlight created a shaft of brightness in the center of the aisle, picked out by whirling dust particles that rose in twisting motes from the floorboards. The constant motion of the Pullman car caused this as a powerful 4-6-2 Baldwin locomotive pulled the train through the Texas Panhandle. Rebecca Caldwell sat in a plush upholstered seat on the shady side of the carriage.

Her destination was Austin, the state capital, then on to San Antonio. There she would meet her stepson, Joey Ridgeway. She had not seen Joey in nearly two years. The last time he had run away from the Parsons' farm with Winnona, both of them infatuated and determined to get married and shape a new life together. Joey had barely turned fourteen at the time, Winnona a year younger. The hardships and travails of their journey across the Staked Plains of Texas, and the stern lecture from Rebecca, had disabused the youngsters of their grand design. Winnona went back to her widowed mother's farm. Joey had been admitted to a well respected academy for young gentlemen in San Antonio.

Oh, my, what a change for that young man, Rebecca considered. The straw-haired youngster had swum buck naked in the creek on his father's ranch in Montana, lived with and as an Oglala Sioux in the camp of Iron Calf, and discovered rather early the forbidden joys of sex on the Parsons' farm. How different the discipline and regimen of an all male institute of higher learning.

It probably bored him to distraction, she realized. That was the main reason behind this trip. She would take Joey to the Gulf Coast, for a couple of weeks to fish, swim, explore and generally let him burn up his boyish energy in a manner more in keeping with his past. Why, then, did she feel a certain unease at setting the plan in motion?

Joey had thrived on life in the Sioux camp, as had she for five long years. Vivid memories washed up out of storage as the miles slid by outside the train. Clearly, as though it had happened yesterday, Rebecca saw her arrival in the Oglala village at the tender and impressionable age of 14.

For nearly two years, Rebecca lived in isolation and misery. She hated being there, she refused at first to learn the language and was treated shabbily by all in general. She hated it more to learn the shameful truth that Iron Calf was her father. She found that fact particularly ironic since she and her mother had come to the camp as the result of being traded to Iron Calf by Bitter Creek Jake Tulley and his outlaw gang. Rebecca discovered to her horror that these desperados included her uncles, Virgil and Ezekial Caldwell. Then, quite suddenly, Rebecca's status in the band changed . . .

"I see you," the handsome youth began quite shyly.

"I see you," Rebecca Caldwell responded in the

Lakota tongue. Only six months had gone by since she had relented and used the language. "Go away," she went on in a scolding tone. "I'm washing myself."

"I know you are," Four Horns responded. "I came to clean up, too."

"I know who you are," Rebecca threatened. He was less than two years older than she, and clearly the handsomest boy in camp. "You're supposed to wash where the other boys do."

A smile played on Four Horns' full, sensuous lips. He looked at the highlights that water put in Rebecca's raven locks. "When we are little, we swim together and bathe together," he stated factually. "It's only after a boy's dreaming time and a girl goes to talk with the *pezuta-wicasa* that custom says we must be apart until we are husband and wife."

"I will not be your wife!" Rebecca disclaimed hotly. She carefully evaded the fact that she had never visited the healer and learned the secrets of a Sioux woman. "I will not be wife to any dirty *Oglalahca!*"

Laughing, Four Horns toed-off his moccasins and removed his loincloth. He revealed a partly erect organ that rose from a sparse tuft of silken black hairs. Despite her anger, Rebecca could not take her eyes off the instantly tantalizing object.

"That's why I wanted to take a bath," Four Horns informed her through his chuckle. "So I could prove to you that I am not a 'dirty' Oglala."

With that, he dove into the water. Rebecca uttered a small squeak of outrage and surprise that he would be so bold. Still, the memory of that enlarging tube of flesh persisted and made her groin tingle. Water swirled around her loins and Four Horse broke the surface of the creek in a cloud of droplets. With a whoosh of exuberance he rose to his full height before her.

He stood barely six inches away, yet with both hands up, unfastening his braids, he still managed to touch her with . . . with *something*. A thrill of excitement ran through Rebecca's slender frame when she realized what part of him prodded her lower belly.

Throat and mouth suddenly dry, she croaked her reply, rather than producing the soft tone of reason and appeal she wished for.

"We can't be . . . can't do this. If we're—we're caught, we'll be shamed in front of the council and the whole band."

"I don't care. I love you, *Šinaskawin*. I have loved you for two whole years," Four Horns pleaded in a lovesick tone.

"Don't call me that!" Rebecca snapped. "I—I hate that—"

Suddenly she found she did not hate her Lakota name, White Robe Woman. *Šinaskawin* sounded lovely when it came from *his* lips, so close to her own. How could she not be thrilled by the sound of it when that rigid part of him pressed so tightly against her skin above the top of her nearly hairless cleft?

Rebecca shivered and tried to force away her roiled emotions. That only made it worse. For she had caused his secret part to insinuate itself between her legs. It rubbed against the sensitive places on her thighs and she felt so—so wonderful!

"I will come and play my flute outside your lodge," Four Horns proclaimed his adoration. "I will bring my buffalo robe and we can sit and watch the stars. I will bring all the ponies I have to Iron Calf so I may claim your love."

Fighting her inner turmoil, Rebecca pushed him back. "You'll not do any of those things. I forbid—I don't want—I can't . . ." Her protests ran out.

Four Horns produced a boyish grin. "I will tell you what I shall do. Tonight I will come to your lodge. I will slip under the skirt and find your sleeping space. Then we will do what a man and a woman do in the night."

"You're horrible," Rebecca sqeaked, yet for some reason the prospect excited her. "We would be found out. You—I—we would make noises, wake my mother and the old woman."

"No, little one. Your father built a small lodge for you. Even though you do not use it often, tonight you will sleep there, alone. I will come to you."

He left her then, her mind completely confused. In a pensive mood, Rebecca finished her bath and climbed from the water to dry herself. A troop of small boys, all quite naked and bearing willow branch fish traps, rounded a bend. When they saw her they put hands to their mouths and ran off giggling.

For all her admonitions not to cooperate in any way with Four Horns' mad design, nighttime found Rebecca settled down alone in her little lodge beside the large tipi of Iron Calf and the medium sized one of his two lesser wives, one of which was Rebecca's mother. Rebecca's heart beat rapidly and she frequently caught herself listening intently for some sound that would betray the approach of her would-be lover.

No stranger to arousal, for the past eight years she had found a variety of means to extract secret pleasure from her body, Rebecca veritably vibrated with expectation. He wouldn't come. No—no, he would and she would send him packing for his gall. No, he

9

would touch her, they would kiss, hold each other under a buffalo robe. Slowly they would remove their clothing. She had purposely gone to bed dressed instead of in her usual nude condition. And they would explore the angles and depressions of each other's body. Then, he would join with her and give her that thrill beyond all expectation.

Her thoughts continued in a confused, steamy whirl until the last camp dog stopped its yapping and settled for the night. Still no sign of Four Horns. Then she heard a faint scratching on the scraped hide cover of the lodge. Her breath caught. Only a faint glow of the dying embers illuminated the interior. Straining, Rebecca at last made out a bronze hand under the edge of the skirt.

Slowly the pliable material rose to reveal the dark silhouette of a person lying on one side. A long moment went by, filled with her rapid heartbeats, then the figure scooted inside and the skirt lowered. Four Horns found her at once. They embraced soundlessly, though with mutual ardor. In an instant his hands were all over her; gentle, curious, yet insistent.

To her surprise, Rebecca found that she, too, ran her fingers over his smooth, coppery skin. The touch of a rigid stub of nipple against the palm of her right hand sent a stab of dizzy sensation through her body. His breath came hot and irregular against her ear.

"I knew you'd be here, I knew it," he whispered. "Oh, this is so wonderful, *Sinaskawin*. I've longed for you, ached, dreamed. I — I've even released my sap to the ground imagining this moment."

His confession shocked her. "Why? How? How could that be?"

"In my weakness I resorted to the pastime of small boys. Young men on the verge of being warriors do

10

not take themselves in hand."

To Rebecca's reckoning it came out sounding arrogant, yet at the same time self-conscious, and a terrible pun. It made her giggle. Suddenly the last barrier of her reticence broke down.

"Would you be shamed by it if—if I—if I t-took you in hand?"

Four Horns all but yelped from the euphoria he felt as she matched actions to words. The presence of her small hand under his loincloth sent gooseflesh over the young Oglala's hide. Instinct, rather than knowledge, guided Rebecca in her exploration and execution. Rough and irregular at first, her stroke smoothed into an eons old rhythm that soothed yet excited her youthful partner.

For a long while they lay together on the soft robes while Rebecca perfected her newfound talent. A welling urgency deep within prompted her to speak at last. "Well, is this all?"

"Uh—no—no, I can—we can—ah," Four Horns' voice broke off, betraying his own inexperience.

Rebecca stopped manipulating him and raised to her knees. Slowly she pulled up her elk-hide dress. Once more, Four Horns experienced the thrill of seeing her magnificent body. He licked his dry lips and fought to break his gaze away from the firm, full globes of her breasts, the nipples impudently thrust upward. She trembled as he roused himself and took off his loincloth. Now fully erect, his organ rose in a sweeping arc from his groin.

Wonder of wonders. *This* was what she had been holding, stroking only moments before. A hot flash burned through Rebecca's torso and tingled her fingers and toes. Impulsively she reached out to encircle the heated flesh of his swaying member.

Shyly, Four Horns reached out to her nearly hairless mound. His fingers darted nervously as he cat-walked them along the moist outer fringe of her cleft. Rebecca sighed and moaned. He hesitantly inserted a digit. Rebecca wanted to scream with happiness.

"Oh, F-Four Horns, I — I'm on fire. I'm burning," she panted.

"So am I. By all the spirits, you are so lovely."

Whirling in the rapture of their explorations they went on for a long, satisfying time. Once more they lay full length, each desiring that every possible bit of tingling skin made contact with the beloved flesh of the other. When at last the splendorous moment came, after unbearable excitation, Rebecca barely felt the momentary sharp pain that signaled the devastation of her maidenhead as Four Horns pierced her veil and plunged to the depths.

Nothing would ever be the same again, Rebecca thought frantically. Who would want it to be? a part of her asked giddily. To go back would be to live without this most perfect of all human endeavors. How could anything feel so good? She seemed to swell up and burst. Four Horns' mouth worked in silent howls of joy and he shuddered his way to completion.

For both of them the first time had ended too soon. Avidly, and completely without shame or self-consciousness, Rebecca went about arousing Four Horns for another tantalizing excursion into the field of Eros. She could not get enough of his hard fullness churning within her. For his part, Four Horns would have given away everything he owned to be able to continue this most splendorous of contests forever. Between bouts they vowed to be discreet after this first discovery of their compatibility. Each promised to abide by the customs of the people, only

12

to lose themselves in another frenzy of ardor. It went on nearly all night. . . .

"Oh, my," Rebecca Caldwell blurted aloud. Her cheeks burned, her heart fluttered and a giddy sensation revealed how excited her remembering had made her. She would have to stop that. Not a chance that this trip would put her in the way of anyone who could make the inner fires blaze the way Four Horns had.

Or would it? Her gaze took in a tall, handsome man who had entered the car and strode down the aisle toward her seat. He had the lithe grace of a cougar and the total awareness of his surroundings of a Sioux brave. To add to the disconcerting image, he looked directly at her. The expression was one of appreciation and blatant interest.

So far fall's splendor of reds, golds and palest yellows had not touched the cottonwood trees within this sheltered draw along Bluff Creek in south-central Kansas. A high ridge—the bluffs that provided the name for the meandering stream—formed a wind and weather break to the north and northwest. Corresponding to that, a low swale gave generous southern exposure. Only a few miles from Indian Territory, actually a part of it until the Kansas Nebraska Act of 1856, it had proven bountiful farmland. All of nature seemed to hold its breath as an orange crescent peeped over a knoll to the east. For once the nearly unceasing winds of the Kansas prairie had calmed to a gentle zephyr.

Oddly enough, this respite did not bring along with it the usual plethora of bird song, insect hum and rustle of small animals. An eerie silence hung over the farm. Suddenly the pigs set up a wild

13

squeal, two milk cows lowed in alarm and the geese in the farmyard squawked their warnings of strangers. The farmer, a leathery faced individual, long, lean and only slightly bent by the plow, looked around in surprise. On his way to the barn to begin his early morning round of chores, he had a slop bucket in each hand.

They fell to the ground and spilled their contents as three arrows pierced his body. He screamed hideously as he dropped to his knees, then sprawled in the slop, twitching his way into death. A piercing feminine shriek came from the farmhouse. The cracking voice of a teenaged boy shouted alarm from the barn. Pandemonium seized the family as Kiowa braves, led by Big Belly, surged into the open space between barn and house.

Another youth, barely into his teens, blasted two of the Indians with a shotgun and slammed shut the door to the house. From the barn came pitiful cries as the Kiowa warriors tended to the boy's older brother. Immediately shutters slammed closed on the windows. Biting her lip, the mother of this brood of nine children took up a rifle and poked the muzzle from one firing slit in the thick wooden slabs at one window. The boy fired another round from the Parker and reloaded automatically. Three small girls huddled in one corner by the fireplace and whimpered.

"Take the stinking meat out of there," Big Belly commanded, referring to the cattle, "then burn the place."

Howling warriors obeyed, driving the cattle from the barn. Big Belly pointed to the house. "Set fires. Drive out the white worms."

Half a dozen Kiowas rushed the house. The shotgun boomed again and again, the rifle cracked. Four men lay writhing on the ground. Big Belly didn't like the danger this represented for his men. He signaled to Red Hawk.

"Make firebrands. I want you to charge the house with four men. Then I want you . . ." Quickly he outlined the rest of his plan.

During the long ride, Rebecca Caldwell had an opportunity to do more than reflect on those few happy years she shared with Four Horns in the Oglala camp. She observed her fellow passengers—watching people had become a habit to her in her years of searching for the men repsonsible for her mother's insanity and death in the Sioux village and her own degradation both before and after her brief time with Four Horns. In particular, she observed the activities of two gentlemen who radiated an aura of confidence and respectability.

They dressed well, if not expensively, and had polished manners and a smooth, controlled grace to their movements. From experience she knew the type well and soon sized them up as cowmen. An opportunity to verify her evaluation came shortly before noon on the second day of the journey. The two suave fellows settled in with a graying man and his wife, obviously prosperous ranchers from the Panhandle. The elder of the pair began his pitch in a tone so low Rebecca barely made out the words.

"Excuse me, sir, ma'am. I don't wish to intrude," the oily voice purred. "It's just that . . . well, we have a problem. Ah! Forgive me. Let me introduce myself and my colleague. I am Martin Bowers and this is Albert Graham. We are Railroad Inspectors."

"Sam Varney," the portly, well-dressed rancher replied. "This is m'wife, Mildred. Work for the rail-

15

road, eh? Don't mean to pry, but what exactly is this problem of yours?"

"Well, sir, it pains me to say this, but we suspect one of the express agents of not being entirely honest. Truth to tell, we have reason to believe he has been stealing sums of money from mail and passenger deposits in the company safe up in the express car."

Mildred Varney put a hand to her mouth. "Why, that's terrible," she gasped.

"Hush, Milly, let the man explain," Sam Varney admonished his wife.

"The thing is, we need a means to prove what, for now, we only suspect."

Sam raised an eyebrow. "I reckon those suspicions are mighty strong or you wouldn't be discussing it with an outsider."

Bowers put on an expression of surprised respect. "You're a perceptive man, Mr. Varney."

"Thank you. Call me Sam. Only handle I've answered to for years now."

"All right, Sam. You hit that right on the head. Now here's what Mr. Graham and I have decided to do. With nothing but suspicions that this agent is stealing funds from the mail and strongbox, we want to bring him out in the open. If you good folks would assist us, I'm sure we could manage that. In the process we can catch the villain red-handed. All it will take is a few—ah—thousand dollars cash, marked in a suitable manner, and put in an envelope.

"In turn, we will take that envelope to a trusted employee in the express car. After he receives it, he will drop a remark about a lot of loose cash on this run in the hearing of our suspect. When the train reaches Austin, his part of the run is over. Once he leaves the train, Mr. Graham and I will nab him and confront him with the evidence. Then, of course," Bowers paused and shrugged his shoulders, arms at his waist, in a palms up gesture, "we'll return the money to its rightful owner."

"I — ah — ummmm," Sam Varney mulled it over. "Railroad Inspectors, eh? I suppose you have some identification? A badge, maybe?"

"Why, certainly. My fault for not showing you our credentials earlier. Here you are."

Bowers and Graham produced badges pinned to tooled leather flaps and from their wallets cards embossed with the railroad's name and logo and typed names and descriptions of the bearers. Sam Varney studied them through a pair of half-lens spectacles he fished from his coat pocket.

"Looks all right," he allowed after a moment. "Now, supposin' we go along with you? How do we set this up?"

One of the oldest games in the confidence man's repertoire, Rebecca Caldwell thought, incensed. She wondered how many others they had managed to fleece so far. By her own count she had seen them make their pitch to at least five other individuals or couples. They didn't seem to single out only well-to-do victims. They were most liberal in their gain of ill-gotten goods. She should give it some thought, Rebecca decided.

Before this train ride ended, she felt sure she might be able to do something about these silky criminals. Something decidedly fatal to them if they chose to resist.

2

Frustrated by the stoutly built farmhouse, which was half-soddy, the Kiowas had been forced to continue their attack on the Kansas farm into late afternoon. Gunfire from the house kept them at bay far longer than Big Belly had expected. Every attempt at rushing the structure failed. Fall sun beat down on the corpses in the yard, white and red men alike. At last Big Belly called Red Hawk to him again.

"This is taking too long," the war chief declared. "We must do something to stop it."

"We have tried . . ." Red Hawk began weakly.

"We will try again," Big Belly snapped. "This time I want you to mount up and circle the house, confuse them as to where the attack will come. Then I will send warriors with firebrands. When they are shot at, they will fall, whether they are hit or not. After that . . ."

To his great satisfaction, the ruse worked perfectly, Big Belly noted some twenty minutes later. Out of five braves, three lay unharmed, though apparently dead, within ten paces of the house. Their firebrands still crackled on the hard-packed dirt.

"Now, ride around them again," he commanded Red Hawk.

18

When the howling Kiowas formed a curtain of dust with their swift ponies, Big Belly blew on a small wooden pipe. At his signal, the "dead" men rose and rushed the house. One got in close and poked his rifle barrel through a firing slit in one shutter.

A charge of nails belched from the trade rifle and flayed the face of the fourteen year old who had proven so far to be an outstanding marksman. He fell dead in a welter of blood. A younger brother, a boy of eleven, took up the dead lad's position and blasted the killer with a load of 00 Buckshot. The others managed to evade him, and toss their firebrands onto the roof. Flames began to spread on the dry wood shingles.

"Good, good," Big Belly said to himself. "Try them again," he urged.

The younger boy's aim proved less accurate than his older brother. He missed one shot entirely, only wounded with the second barrel and paused to reload. Smoke sank into the rooms from the burning roof. When flames licked through the ceiling, one of the girls could bear it no longer.

Screaming hysterically, she ran to the back door and flung it open. Two Kiowas appeared in the doorway at once. They threw her aside and entered, killing as they advanced from room to room. In no time the slaughter ended and the lusty rapes began. Only sobs and howls of pain rose above their grunts and laughter.

Rebecca Caldwell had lunch with Carlton Blake. They dined in a small depot café while the Texas & Pacific locomotive took on water and fuel. Their conversation remained trivial until near time to reboard the train. Then Carlton grew serious.

"This has been most pleasant. I would feel even more flattered and fortunate if you would agree to dinner tonight. We'll be in Austin some time tomorrow," he added, which foretold a parting.

"There is a layover for both of us there," Rebecca reminded him. "Your train to Galveston and mine to San Antonio won't leave until the next day."

"So what are you suggesting?" Carl asked and Rebecca noted the anticipation in the tone of his voice.

His smile, while boyish, held a heavy, devil-may-care maturity that tugged at Rebecca's deepest drives. Impulsively she reached over and patted his hand. "Why, then, surely it will be far more elegant dining in Austin than along the track somewhere."

"Indeed. And I have every intention of seeing you around town to a fine dinner while we wait for our other trains. Yet, tonight we could best pass the time in maintaining our cordial acquaintance."

"You are eloquent," Rebecca said candidly. "And you've made your point. I accept. Dinner it is."

"You have truly made my day," Carlton beamed.

Rebecca noted a slight, giddy lift as she set about her other project for the afternoon. She located the bunco steerers in the smoking car at the rear of the train. Rebecca approached them with a tentative, nervous smile.

"Excuse me, gentlemen," she began as they rose politely to acknowledge the presence of a lady. "I certainly don't wish to make the impression that I have pursued you here. True, I've been looking for you . . ."

"Why is that?" the one who called himself Graham asked bluntly.

"Earlier, before our noon stop, I couldn't help but overhear a portion of your conversation with Mr. and Mrs. Varney. I gather from what I heard that there is something amiss—wrong on this train?"

Each of the con men, Fletcher Griffin and Nathan Benjamin, studied the earnest young lady who stood at their minute, round scrap of a table, a small tapestried purse clutched in her hands. Her expensive, new clothing, excellent grooming and natural poise indicated at least some fair standard of wealth. A silent exchange established a consensus. They might as well make one more score.

Benjamin cleared his throat. "This is Mr. Graham, I'm Bowers. We're agents—ah—inspectors for the Texas and Pacific Railroad. You are a most perceptive young woman, Miss—aaah—?"

"Rebecca Caldwell. Is it something serious? Is there anything I can do to help?"

"Yes to both, Miss Caldwell," Griffin injected.

Quickly they went through their story and laid heavily upon her ability, no matter how limited in available funds, to help catch the culprit. Rebecca fought to maintain an ingenuous expression of gullibility and made answer most often with nods of her pretty head. When the pitch concluded, Rebecca asked for the expected verification, and saw their credentials. Then she put forward all the right questions, with an emphasis on how the money should be marked and what to put on the envelope.

They responded with alacrity, in conspiratorially low voices. A sum of three hundred dollars, a munificent amount for a woman traveling alone in that country, was agreed upon. Bowers and Graham wanted her to take care of it immediately and pass the money on to them. With her dinner date in mind, and a desire to make sure they took all the bait, and the hook, she stalled.

"I'll have to obtain the money from among my—er—delicate garments, gentlemen. So that will take

21

some time. Shall we meet after dinner tonight? Say, here in the smoking car or on the observation platform out there?"

"Excellent, excellent. You seem to have a talent for this clandestine work, Miss Caldwell," Benjamin flattered her unblushingly.

"Oh, you'd be surprised, Mr. Bowers," Rebecca could not resist injecting.

Pony Nose looked at the bleak vista of the sandy soil and stunted scrub of this land called the Indian Nations. This was not his people's home. Once the brave people of the *Suhtaila*—the People of the Ridge—lived free and wandered all the great plains from the Yellow Rock country to the Black Hills, the Grandmother Land to the Fat Meat river. They feasted with their cousins the Lakota, danced to honor their Father Sun together with many tribes.

Now we have only this small piece of barren soil that would not feed a single bison, he thought wistfully. Blue Star grows weary here, her face is becoming lined and sunken like an old person's. Only the oldest of his three children remembered the lush, verdant place where they lived before. Eleven summers the slim little boy had seen, his face sweet with radiant love and total trust. Yet even he has begun to show the ravages of the hostile southern land.

Willow Leaf was a baby, still on a cradle board, when the white soldiers moved them south. She remembers nothing but want, cold and hunger. Sweet Water was born in this emptiness. A boy without a past, without a home. Love poured from the heart of Pony Nose for his wife and children. Would they ever know the free life? Would any of them?

Walks Proud was right. We must no longer endure the chains and shame of the white men. Tall and

22

well-muscled, in his prime only a season past thirty summers, Pony Nose ran a hand that trembled slightly over his broad, flat face, down the hawk beak of his nose. Squinting at the setting sun, Pony Nose turned back to the scant band of Cheyenne young men who waited his decision in varying states of eager anticipation or bleak resignation.

"We will do it. We will fight. Tonight we ride out! Walks Proud carries the war pipe for all of us. I have spoken," Pony Nose stated, his voice rising in pitch and volume as he made his declaration.

Dinner turned out to be delightful. The depot in Abilene, Texas sported a first-class restaurant, rather than a hot lunch, hurry-up counter. Fresh antelope steak, steaming parsley potatoes and a choice from a dozen side dishes made it by far the best meal since departing from Amarillo. Pies baked that day, three puddings and a cheese board rounded out the sumptuous repast. It put Carlton Blake in an expansive mood. He collared a freckle-faced youngster and offered him a handsome tip of a quarter if he could round up a small flask of good brandy, naming three French brands to select from, and sent the lad scurrying off to locate the elegant liquor.

"I thought we might enjoy it later this evening. Once we're back on the train," he told Rebecca. "We could watch the stars from the observation platform, sip a little brandy and . . ." He searched about the station, saw a small alcove counter with gold foil wrapped sweets, "some of those chocolates. It would give us a chance to get to know each other more."

"I—I'd love to," Rebecca stammered, painfully aware of her scheduled meeting with the bunco steerers on that same platform. "Though I don't know to what end. You'll be taking a different train from

23

Austin to Galveston."

"I've decided to go on to San Antonio and then to Galveston," Carlton cut her short. "I don't know why. Perhaps the company I'm keeping." His eyes glowed and he smiled warmly.

Confronted by that, Rebecca didn't know how to reply, except to blurt the truth, or something close to it. "I—I can't. I—I've something I must take care of first. B-but I can see you later on. Will that be all right?"

His feelings wounded, Carlton produced a pained expression and then put on the best front the circumstances allowed. "I suppose it will. It'll have to. I've not . . . there isn't something I've done or said . . . ?"

Recovered, Rebecca put a hand on his arm. "Of course not, Carl. And I truly regret I can't go out there with you right after the train starts off. Give it two hours and I'll be delighted to go."

Twenty minutes after the T&P Limited got under way, Carlton sat in his Pullman car with a copy of the Abilene newspaper, opened to an inner page, his entire view of the car ostensibly blocked. When Rebecca went by him, he lowered the upper edge enough to peer over it at her departing back. Carl laid aside the newspaper and rose to follow her.

To his consternation she went directly to the smoking lounge car and paused to address one of a pair of sharpies he had noted earlier. Rebecca's furtive meeting with the younger of the two bunco steerers made it more to his interest. Curiosity bridling him, he stepped back into the shadows of the vestibule until Rebecca and the con man went through the door onto the observation platform. Did she work with them?

Carl Blake rejected the idea out of hand. He

24

waited long enough to satisfy himself that no one else would be joining them, then edged forward to a place he could watch through a window draped with heavy curtains. Disappointment pinched a furrow between his eyebrows. With all the confounded train noise, it would be impossible to hear what they were saying. Or even to have much warning if she was in danger.

"You brought the money with you?" the man who called himself Griffin asked tensely.

"Yes I did," Rebecca answered.

"I have an envelope ready," Graham/Griffin responded.

"Well, I," Rebecca hesitated, sliding a hand into her tapestry purse.

From the shadow under the overhang Benjamin's deep voice prodded, "Be quick about it. We won't have another chance to plant the envelope before the train reaches Austin."

"Is that so, Mr. Bowers? I was about to say that I've decided not to give you the money. Further, I think it would be an excellent idea for you to return the money to all the marks you have taken or be prepared to suffer the consequences."

"*What?* What are you talking about?" Griffin demanded. "See here, Miss, we're agents of the Texas and Pacific Railroad and . . ."

"You are," Rebecca interrupted, "con men. Bunco steerers might be a better name. You've been bilking people on this train with a clever twist on the "Pigeon Drop," six I know of. So, give back all the money to all your victims and I might be persuaded to not turn you over to the police when we reach Austin."

"Don't be ridiculous, my dear," Bowers/Benjamin rumbled affably. "Whoever would believe you. Our

25

credentials are quite genuine, I assure you. The man who provided them for us is an expert. Consider how it would look to the authorities. Your word against ours. You, a young woman, traveling alone, who made indecent and immodest proposals to us and then threatened to cause us much harm and embarrassment if we refused to pay you a substantial sum of money."

"It won't work, Bowers, or whatever your name happens to be. I made a note of every man or couple you told your tale to. If they don't have their money back," Rebecca went on with growing confidence, "I'm sure they'll scream loud and long."

"You're being absurd," Bowers assured her. "No one likes admitting he's been made a fool of. They won't say a word. We can accept omitting your little nest egg from our take, but I would suggest it would be far healthier for you to keep your pretty little mouth shut."

"Yes," Griffin hissed, "I'd listen to him if I were you. It would be a simple matter to take care of you, with no one the wiser."

"Don't threaten me, you weasel," Rebecca grated. "It might not be as simple as you think."

Griffin shrugged. "Why not? All we'd have to do is throw you headfirst off this speeding train and you'd be tomorrow's old news."

Rebecca looked at the smug, well fed, snappy dresser. His long, wavy, blond hair ruffled in the gusts of wind from the train. What had before been clear, candid blue eyes now held a dark malevolence rarely encountered in confidence men. It gave her a cold chill, which she cast off with a roll of her shoulders. Forcing a nasty smile, she extended her purse a few inches.

"I am sorry you had to complicate matters like

that," she told him. "We could have ended this without any harm being done to anyone."

"Cut the bullshit, sister," Griffin snarled. Even his partner winced at his crudity. "You do it our way or we feed your cute little ass to the coyotes."

"I think not," Rebecca icily defied him. "You know, this purse only cost a dollar. Sacrificing it by blowing a hole through the bottom would be worth the price to get to watch the expression on your face while you die. Most connivers are cowards at heart. Violence is not a part of their way. You are of a kind that should be rooted out of the breed before you do some real harm."

Griffin desperately tried to regain control of the situation. "You're all mouth, sister. That gun's a bluff too. Probably a comb."

Rebecca licked her lips in a manner that under other circumstances could be considered sensual. It only served to give Fletcher Griffin a flash of deep, genuine fear. "I stopped counting after the seventh man I killed," Rebecca told him. "That was my no-good, outlaw uncle, Virgil Caldwell. Since then," she shrugged, "there must have been forty more."

Goaded by fear and loathing, Griffin darted a hand under his coat to where a soft leather pouch held his hide-out gun. He came free with the little .32 five-shot Spaulding a fraction of a second before a fist-sized portion of the bottom of Rebecca's purse disintegrated and sprayed toward his face.

A lance of flame followed, smoke quickly obscuring the scene. A sharp, stabbing pain in his right shoulder informed Fletcher Griffin of the .38 slug from Rebecca's Smith & Wesson Baby Russian. Nerveless fingers released his own pipsqueak revolver and he staggered backward.

"Jesus, I'm shot! She shot me, Nathan," Griffin

27

wailed.

At that moment, Carlton Blake came through the heavy metal door, a short-barrel Colt .45 in his fist, hammer back and ready to fall. "Do something," he barked at Nathan Benjamin, "and I'll splatter your brains all over the canopy."

A green tinge formed a circle around Nathan Benjamin's mouth as his face drained gray-white. His thick lips formed an "Oh" and he kept both hands clearly in sight of the coach lamps to either side of the door. Carlton gestured with the short barrel of his revolver.

"Now what?" he asked Rebecca.

Unruffled, Rebecca answered, "We take them to the conductor and have him lock them up somewhere. Then in the morning you and I can have loads of fun asking them questions and recovering the money they've cheated out of the marks they took on the train."

"You are amazing," Carlton said with sincere meaning as they herded the crestfallen pair through the cars toward the conductor's station. "How did you know? More so, how and why did you decide to do something about it by yourself?"

"I'm . . . used to such things, Carl. Remind me to tell you about it some time and I will."

"Like while we keep close company on the journey to San Antonio?"

"It could be arranged."

Wincing, Griffin spoke through his pain. "We're not done with you yet, bitch."

It earned him a love tap from the fat butt of Carl's Colt's Sheriff's Model '74. Cringing, the bunco steerer avoided producing any excuse for a repeat performance. The conductor received the con men gratefully and stored them in a locked room usually reserved for replacement crew.

"Well, the suckers will get their money back," Carlton summed up. "What about us?"

"You really want to know?" Rebecca teased lightly. "I for one could use a swallow or two of that brandy."

"So could I. Also a look at those stars with you close by my side."

"I'll drink to that," Rebecca riposted with a merry tinkle of laughter.

Three hundred miles north of Abilene, Texas, in the magenta, umber and yellow arroyos and gullies carved eons ago by the rapid courses of glacial meltwater, life moved at a different pace than in civilized parts. On this night, in one particular arroyo, throbbing drums and the falsetto wail of singers set the tempo. Hard-faced young Cheyenne and Comanches sat around an outdoor council fire.

This, like all of Indian Territory, was supposed to be land in which they were free to roam. Lately, an officious and unduly concerned government in Washington had decided to designate reservation boundaries and confine the varying tribes to the one assigned them. These youthful warriors, albeit untried ones, strongly resented this restriction of movement. How could they hunt? How could they teach their children the ways of the people?

Facing them now, a gaunt young man in a bearhead mask purported to have the answer. His moccasins and loincloth marked him as a Kiowa. His light skin and, had they been able to see it, yellow-streaked, dark brown hair gave rise to doubts of the purity of his blood. None of this mattered, though, as he addressed them in a hypnotic, singsong tone.

"Who among us does not know of the many broken promises and betrayals by the white men? You of the Red Earth People, what of Black Kettle? Did not Yellow Hair meet with him at Council Grove and again at Medicine Lodge and convince him that his people would be safe and live in peace along the Washita? And then that winter did not the same Yellow Hair ride down on the village while the men were hunting and kill the women, children and elderly?"

Angry mutters rose among the assembled Cheyenne. Most had not been born, or were only infants when the dishonorable, scheming liar, Custer, had induced Black Kettle to move his people into a perfect, remote spot, far from any unbiased observers, for the planned slaughter of that winter. The story had been repeated every winter in the lodges and now they lusted for revenge. Some, they knew, had already tasted of the sweet fruit of vengeance.

"You Comanche," Walks Proud challenged. "What happened to your reservation on the Staked Plains? It was to be yours 'for as long as the grass is green.' Now you are here, living on less land than your villages covered before."

Dark scowls lined the faces of the Comanches. They, too, murmured heatedly over the perfidy of the white man. Several uttered brief yips and howls that signified a desire to fight.

"The food we were promised, where is it? When it does come, the cattle are scrawny — if there are any at all — the flour full of little creatures and sand, the corn is shriveled and spotted with mold. If, I say again, if it comes at all! What of the white man's yellow metal we are promised, the money? You know where it goes, same as I. Into the pockets of the soldier chiefs and the Indian agents. The 'poor savages can't be trusted with money.' They 'don't know the value and how to use it.' I say better we misuse it than have it stolen from us before we even hold it in our hands."

An utter silence, more ominous than the throbbing drums, gripped the audience. Walks Proud paced back and forth before them, arms folded over his flat, smooth chest. Oddly colored yellow eyes glittered at the young men from within the bear mask He raised his arms high above his head and the drums throbbed.

"Join me, my brothers! My medicine is strong. I have taken up the war pipe and call on all of strong heart to come clasp it and follow me. I will lead you to the ultimate victory over the whites. Those who ride the war trail with me will push the whites back across the big river, back beyond the blue ridged mountains far to the home of the sun. We will drive the hated whites back into the great water out of which our Father Sun awakens each day.

"Let them swim to their tribes beyond the great waters!" he concluded in a burst of energy.

Whoops and howls answered him. Individuals rose and began to stamp out the intricate steps of the war dance. Others kept time by clapping. A few lusty voices joined in a song of valor known to all plains tribes.

"Already your Kiowa brothers are seeking the white enemy in the north. They have struck and tasted white blood, taken scalps. Who among our Cheyenne brothers does not know the name of Pony Nose? Cheyenne Dog Soldiers under Pony Nose have also raided against the hateful whites.

"They go with my blessing," Walks Proud told them, then paused to draw a deep breath. "Their medicine, my medicine, is strong! The way clear!

32

Victory assured!" His voice had risen to an hysterical pitch. "Do you want proof? I'll show you the power that comes from my prayers and fasting." Walks Proud bent low and opened a parfleche bag. From it he extracted a human head.

"This is the head of the great Indian fighter, Harlan Carruthers," he announced. The grisly trophy hung from his clinched fist by the hair, the skin bloated and gray-green, mottled with black. "If the Gray Ghost cannot prevail against me, who can?"

Cheering, the men queued up to pledge their allegiance while the big drums throbbed and those already enlisted began to dance.

Austin, Texas, sprawled in the throes of a growth spurt. Reconstruction had lifted its heavy hand of oppression off the Texans' necks with the ratification of the Constitution of 1869, and slowly capital began to accrue among the native land owners. Cattle drives to far off Kansas had brought money back into Texas. The cattlemen reflected their affluence through investments in business and commerce in general. With the growth of the railroads, more cities than Galveston and Houston benefited. When the Texas & Pacific train deposited Rebecca Caldwell and Carlton Blake in Austin they found the usually simple task of obtaining rooms for an overnight stay more complicated than expected.

"We can try the Bullock House," Carlton suggested when they had exhausted the first several hostelries close to the depot. "It's older than these establishments, but comfortable."

"That sounds fine," Rebecca agreed. "Perhaps we can get adjoining rooms?"

Carlton suppressed a grin. "A marvelous idea. We

can refresh ourselves, get a light lunch and see some of the city. Austin has been the state capital for more than a decade. Yet only now is it growing. I think it's exciting."

"You do? Somehow, Carl, I figured you for one who disdained the closeness of civilization, for all your obvious affluence," Rebecca responded.

"Oh, I do. Some of the time, though, I take a lot of pleasure out of the refinements of the world's cultural centers. And," he added with a wink, "I even play a mean game of billiards."

Laughing, they directed their steps toward the Bullock House. They found they could obtain adjoining rooms. The clerk produced a knowing, smug smile, that Rebecca longed to wipe off his face with a punch in the mouth, as he displayed the key to the interconnecting door.

"If you wish this, you need only ask. Otherwise, I will have the bellboy leave the door unlocked and open," the young, slim clerk simpered.

"We'll take the key," Carlton growled.

"Yes," Rebecca added. "We don't consider the state of that door to be any of your business."

A flat, soft, moist palm against the bell striker summoned a red velvet uniformed youth in his pimply mid-teens, who took their luggage, room keys and led the way up a flight of stairs. After gaining entry, he opened wide the spacious windows and accepted a gratuity from Carlton. Once he had departed, Rebecca and Carl doubled over in a fit of laughter.

"What prigs they are," Rebecca managed through a peal of giggles.

"On the contrary," Carlton whooped in a cascade of chuckles, "what dirty little minds they have."

"At least we're here," Rebecca went on, sobering.

34

"We each have a room. I want a long, hot bath."

"I could use that, and the attentions of a barber, too. Let's say I meet you in the lobby in an hour. We'll find an interesting place for lunch, then take a stroll around the capital grounds. The Stephen Fuller Austin mansion has an impressive art collection, I hear."

"Sounds fine," Rebecca relented. He wanted to show her the sites, she would go along. "An hour, then."

Bright and relaxed in fresh clothing, Rebecca descended to the lobby with a quarter hour to spare. Workmen were industrious in their efforts to replace part of the parquet flooring with polished marble in irregular shapes, set in a pure white grout. A faint haze of snowy dust drifted across the horsehair-stuffed wing chairs and casual tables that graced a glassed bow designed for the relaxation of guests. Even the drapes wore a hoary patina.

Amused at this show of ostentation, Rebecca selected a settee that afforded a clear view of the staircase and opened a month-old copy of *Harpers'*. The new fashions startled her. Revealing lace bodices, much lower in cut than the accepted custom abounded among the new gowns. Skirts ended above the ankle, although high, black, button shoes still seemed to be the mode. Rebecca became so absorbed in her study of New York's "best dressed," that she didn't see Carl Blake make a striking entrance on the sweeping arc of the stairs.

His indulgent chuckle made her aware that he stood over her. "I see that New York has its charms, even for you."

"You caught me, Carl. Curiosity, that's all. I'm willing to bet the dowagers of Austin will never be caught dead in such fashions. Too many preachers in

35

this country to ever expect an ankle to be displayed in public. Shall we go?"

"My pleasure, dear Becky." Carl offered her his arm.

Three men lay sprawled and naked by their wagon, five miles inside Indian Territory from the Texas border. The canvas cover had been roughly yanked off to expose the contents. Long wooden cases of rifles and five half barrels of whiskey. Arrows pierced the naked flesh of the dead men. Knives had mutilated the muscles of their arms, opened their bellies, slashed their legs. One had his sex organs cut away and stuffed in his sagging mouth. All had been scalped. A dozen Comanches milled around, waiting for some direction. All thirsted for the taste of the white man's liquor.

"There are bottles here, in boxes," one observed from atop the cargo.

"Look, in here, snake heads, the hot powder of the Mexicans," he listed the contents of a brass bound chest. "Ummm. Tobacco. It is good."

"That means," Stone Knife worked out as he spoke, "that the greedy worms had not mixed up Indian whiskey. It is good. White man's whiskey is clean, does not poison the head or stomach. We will drink this, take some to our brothers. At least they spoke straight about the rifles."

"Ho-ah!" Bright Shield agreed as he opened one crate. "Repeaters. All new and clean. We will kill many whites."

Rapid hoofbeats thundered toward them. "Hurry, take it all," Lame Deer called as he ground to a dusty halt, his stiff-legged pony rolling eyes in protest. "Bluecoats come this way. Hurry, take away the wagon."

Stone Knife nodded his agreement. His lips set in a straight line, thinned by tension and concern, he caught up the reins of his horse and swung onto the flat saddlepad. Lashing the mules, the Comanche warriors set off with their booty. Three warriors remained as a rear guard.

Their brows became daubed with globes of moisture as the hot sun of afternoon grew more intense. They knew their duty, knew how to make fools of the white soldiers. First they rigged braided rawhide ropes to the freshly skinned hide of a horse, weighted it and dragged it off beyond the crest of a rise, obliterating any sign of the wagon's departure. Then they hid themselves as well as the flat terrain would allow. All they had to do was wait until the soldiers came.

Half an hour passed before the patrol's column cantered down on the scene of the killing. The sight of five white bodies lying in the grotesque shape of their agony brought a quick signal to halt.

"My God, sir," the corporal who carried the guidon blurted. "Dirty savages have butchered them." He made a gulping sound and bent sideways from his mount to spew a thick stream of vomit onto the sagebrush.

A moment later a .44-40 slug from one of the recently acquired repeating rifles popped through his skull, cleaning out a portion of his brain along with a spray of blood and fluid. Two more bullets cracked through the air before the dead corporal fell from his horse. A flurry of shouted orders preceded a withering volley of .45-70-405 rounds that raked the ground where powder smoke still hovered.

At once shots came from a different location. More followed from yet another concealed position. Confusion rendered the green troops ineffective.

37

They began to fire wildly, unaimed and far too high. Sudden thudding hoofbeats were felt, more than heard, by the young lieutenant in charge. Rising in his stirrups, completely unafraid of any Indian bullet, he caught sight of a Comanche warrior bent low over the neck of his pony, galloping away from the improvised ambush.

"Hold up. Cease fire! Sergeant, get them stopped."

"Yes, sir. Detail, cease fire!" Half a dozen individual shots answered him. "Goddamnit, I'll break some heads if you don't stop."

More hoofbeats faded in the distance. "Damn, we've lost them, Sergeant," the officer observed.

"That we have, sir. And nothing to tell us which way the others went. They got the wagon, that's for sure."

"Oh, shit! These gun thieves were no loss to humanity, got what they deserve, I'd say," the lieutenant observed. "But those guns, and who knows what else, in the hands of the Comanches is a disaster. It won't look good on my efficiency report."

"Not the sort of thing to build careers on, sir," the sergeant agreed. "And the Colonel's going to be pissed. Do you want me to send a couple of boys ahead to scout out any sign of the wagon?"

"Fat lot of good that will do, Sergeant. They're all green as grass. Most couldn't tell a wagon track from an Injun travois pole mark. Send them anyway. One of them might get lucky."

Lunch had gone well; oysters on the half shell, packed in ice and shipped up from the Gulf in barrels, a clear broth soup, roast grouse stuffed with whole mushrooms and butter. Afterward Rebecca

38

managed to combine business and pleasure by directing their stroll by the railroad freight office so she could check on accommodations for her Palo\se stallion, *Sila*. By three-thirty they had returned to the hotel. Upon entering Rebecca thought she caught a glance of a familiar figure disappearing up the staircase.

"Carl, isn't that . . . ? No, it couldn't be."

"What, Becky?" Carl asked, his mind on a brief snooze after a languorous day.

"I thought I saw that bunco steerer, Nathan Benjamin, climbing the stairs. But the law has him locked away for a while, I'm sure."

"Of course they do. Dinner at eight?"

"Sounds wonderful. Provided I can get unstuffed from lunch. Do they feed like that all the time around here?"

"Politicians, my dear," Carl quipped. "Their appetite for food is as voracious as it is for power and graft. If you want the most of the best, find the restaurants where the politicians eat. I'll see you at seven-thirty."

Dinner proved another feast of gargantuan proportions. Far more than the frugal meals Rebecca usually consumed, she felt stuffed and torpid when they pushed away from the white napery and departed. They found a place to dance. It took only two turns around the floor for Rebecca to discover she trembled with an urgent demand.

Already aroused, the rest of the evening only fueled the growing need that clamored in her loins. When at last they returned to the hotel, Rebecca made hasty excuses to avoid a nightcap in the lobby saloon, and hurried to her room. Alone she undressed and peered at her svelte body in an oval mirror, set in a full-length cherrywood frame. The result was an increase in steamy desire and a slight trembling of her flesh. Fighting her demands, she soon found herself at the connecting door, intent on trying the knob.

If Carl had left it unlocked, she knew he had done so as an invitation. She'd risk being called brazen in order to satisfy the terrible demands of her body. She tried the knob and found solid resistance. A moment of alarm took her hand from it. Silly, she thought. It wasn't that kind of lock. She tried again.

It moved slightly, then stopped against equally firm resistance. She exerted more pressure and, startlingly, the smooth brass bulb began to turn the opposite direction in her hand. With a gasp she jumped back, hand free of the oddly behaving knob and watched wide-eyed as the door opened to reveal a looming figure on the other side . . .

4

Caught!

Rebecca Caldwell's first reaction to the situation came in context of her earlier fancied glance at a man she thought was Nathan Benjamin. Next she thought of her nudity and the awful distance she had to cover to reach her trusty Colt Bisley revolver on the far side of the room. Then a voice came from the dark form.

"You mean . . . that was you trying . . . I thought the damn thing was stuck," Carl Blake blurted out, his voice atremble with an upsurge of laughter.

"Carl? I thought it had some special lock. I wanted . . ." Rebecca rushed without thought. "I mean, I hoped. . . . Oh no, now you've got me all confused.".

"You do know that you're standing there without a stitch on?" Carl broke in, humor still bubbling in his words. "It's rather . . . lovely, I think."

"You're not much better, Carl Blake, standing in that doorway, backlighted by the moon, with only those knee-length drawers on. B-but it's nice, I think," she ended, coyly.

41

"I'm sorry if I frightened you," Carl apologized, not yet making a move to retreat or enter.

"I suppose I would have startled you a good deal more had I gotten through that door in my present condition." Rebecca had to bite down hard to suppress a titter.

"Is it possible we both had the same thing in mind?"

Rebecca gave him a long, head to toe examination through lowered lashes. "Oh, I suspect that might be the case."

"Is this the place where I'm supposed to ask, 'Your room or mine?' " Carl teased.

Rebecca made a low curtsey, miming a full-skirted dress. "Your room, sir. The moonlight is so romantic."

Unstoppably, Carl let a small gasp escape. "My word, you really did have the same idea. C-come on in."

"Shall I bring something? A wrap?" Rebecca asked in a small voice.

"It might be a good idea. Daylight will come eventually," Carl purred.

"You sound rather confident that you can last that long," Rebecca mock challenged.

"I was thinking that you might fall asleep," Carl bantered.

"Beware, my overconfident friend. 'Pride goeth before a fall.' "

"My mother always quoted tidy little homilies like that. I hated it."

To belie his words, Carl took Rebecca in his arms as she neared him and sought her lips with his. Soft and full, they touched his mouth like butterfly wings. Their kiss began gently, growing in force and mobility as their ardor mounted. Carl's left hand

42

splayed between her bare shoulder blades, while the right slid down the tantalizing curve of her back to her small, tight, delightfully rounded bottom.

"Ummmm. Oh, Carl," Rebecca broke their kiss to murmur against him.

She could feel the solid, ample presence of his rigid member, up-curved and pressing against her. Her own heat radiated through the thin cotton cloth of Carl's underdrawers, firing him with greater fervor. They comic-walked into the other room, Carl going backwards. In the center of the worn though still elegant oriental rug, they made a circle in waltz steps and Rebecca began to giggle.

"This is crazy. We never even discussed the possibility. You—you've been so circumspect and . . . well, I began to wonder if you even liked women."

"Fear not, ample evidence of that you will soon see," Carl pontificated like an actor doing Shakespeare.

"Are you going to pull the string?" Rebecca asked through giddy giggles.

"No, I expected that you would."

"Then I shall," she responded eagerly. Her nimble fingers found the bow knot that held his underdrawers tight and yanked a free end with passion driven haste.

Cloth fell away. What the disrobing revealed left Rebecca momentarily speechless. Her jaw sagged, her eyes fixed on a large, rigid wand of truly magic proportions. The thick base of the shaft sprouted from a heavy tuft of fluffy, light brown, curly hair. Upturned and curved to the left, the massive organ swayed without conscious motion on Carl's part. Rebecca bit a lip imagining its power to thrill or to ruin depending on how it was employed. Truly a weapon as well as a treasured toy.

43

"Dear heaven, is that what you've been carting around all this time?" she observed in an attempt to keep the mood light.

"Ummm—yes. It sort of—ah—grows on me," Carl quipped.

A flood of laughter brought relief to the tension his physical endowment had fostered in her. Rebecca hugged him and new bursts of desire spread from the contact of her erect nipples and his hard, silken chest. Carl began to kiss her face, nose, cheeks, forehead, chin, lips. Then on to her ears, down her neck and at last to her breasts.

His teeth nipped at the rosebud of one nipple, then the other, lips fluttering over the sensitive flesh of each lush globe. Moaning softly, Carl began to suck one exquisite mound. His hands continued to explore as did hers. She used both to encircle his rigid member, one above the other. Slowly she stroked him. Rebecca shivered when Carl changed to her other breast.

"You keep that up and you'll get more than you bargained for," she whispered in his ear. "I've been known to lose all restraint."

"One can only hope," Carl released his prize to say.

Then he lifted her in his arms and carried her to the bed. A shaft of moonlight spread across the snowy sheets and turned Rebecca's lightly copper skin to alabaster. Eagerly Carl joined her. For a long time a shower of kisses and caresses covered every inch of their heated flesh. Rebecca found herself with her face close to the broad, flat tip of Carl's prodigious member. She kissed it, licked it, then kissed along the concave upper arc of the shaft, squirmed around and repeated the delirious bussing up the convex lower surface.

44

Carl wriggled and sighed and applied his fingers to her hot, moist cleft, which had bloomed in welcome. His lips fluttered over her thighs. Pressure built for Rebecca and the mindlessness of vigorous passion directed her actions. In a single, swift move she straddled Carl's hips. Carefully she guided his brazen manhood to the fevered nest that longed for its rewarding friction.

Biting her lip, Rebecca lowered her body until the mighty bulb entered her. She gasped and ingested more. Shivers of delight and faint pain radiated through her. She took more and an involuntary wail sped past her lips.

"So much . . . so much," she panted. *It's like having a baby,* she thought, *only in reverse.*

Determination girded her and she enveloped Carl's gargantuan endowment to the hilt. A squeal of joy pierced the air. Then she began to ride him, hips pistoning, breasts swaying, hair loose and flowing. Utterly — utterly unbelievable her mind rejoiced. So good.

"Oooh — sooo — goood!"

On raged the contest, filled with dizzying delights and heady aromas; shivers and gooseflesh came and went. Carl joined his own steady beat to the rhythm of Eros and built new plateaus of euphoria. Time ceased, the moon moved and backlighted Rebecca's surging body. She peaked and peaked again, ground her pubic arch against his until they both hurt and then bucked and swung and drove them on until at last, at long last, the unworldly limbo into which they had been driven burst in mutual release and they sprawled in languid depletion.

"Carl," Rebecca spoke several happy minutes later. "What do you do when you're not sailing a magnificent yacht or making fantastic love?"

45

"I travel, study, sometimes I work at one thing or another."

"You've been to a lot of places?" Rebecca probed.

"Oh, yes. Europe, England, Africa, South America, I've seen at least parts of them all."

"I wondered. You have a slight bit of an accent. I can't quite place it."

"Oxford, I'm afraid, Becky. I matriculated there long enough to receive a Doctor of Letters degree."

"You . . . are an Oxford Don?" Rebecca blurted, surprised.

"Yes, for my sins. It was all a long time ago," Carl admitted.

"It couldn't be too long," Rebecca protested.

"Well, I suppose you're right. It only seems a long time. My striped past makes me sort of an adventurer in the truest sense. At least to some people."

"Really? And what about this luxurious boat you're going to take possession of in Galveston? Your expensive clothes—and at least Oxford explains your genteel way of life—but what do you do to afford all this?"

Carl dismissed his way of living as something he could well afford as a pastime, then concluded, "I came into some money when my parents were killed while I was at Princeton. I invested wisely, went to England and to Oxford, and when I came back I'm afraid I had quite a fortune. So I set off for the good life." He concluded his story with a shrug.

"What are your immediate plans?" An unexplained curiosity goaded Rebecca to ask.

"Nothing certain. Some quiet fishing, a little sailing along the chain of islands off the coast of Texas. Maybe a trip to New Orleans." Carl paused a moment, then went on as though discovering a fresh idea. "Would you like a week in the Vieux Carré?"

"I've been to New Orleans," Rebecca said tightly, bad memories arising of voodoo and danger. "It's not my favorite place. But surely," she went on, rising slightly and playfully taking hold of his relaxed member, "there must be something you can think of doing before all of that?"

"Umm—ahh—yess. Yes, I'm sure I—we—can find something."

By gleeful stages they worked from languor into a frenzy of passion and coupled through the night with erotic abandon.

A flock of crows, boisterous with scolding voices, flew over the large council lodge. A bad sign, Bent Arrow thought. Daytime council meetings had once been the usual. Under the prying eyes of the whites, night had become their friend. Now the seriousness of the issue at hand had demanded a day meeting.

"It is not a good thing," he said aloud to his companion. "The young against the old. It used to be that the hot spirited listened to the advice of their elders. Now they laugh at us and call us old women."

Three Moons worked his mobile face a moment and spat out a gobbet of gristle from the morning's meal. "The young bloods say it is we who give poor counsel. That we have surrendered to the white man's way."

"Yes, I know," Bent Arrow agreed sadly. He glanced around the barren terrain of the Fort Sill reservation and sighed heavily. "I remember going contrary to the wisdom of the council. I was full of vigor and afire with the desire to steal many ponies from the Arapaho and offer them for a good wife. I stated my cause strongly because I wanted to do it so badly. But I listened to the wiser heads, who said to

47

wait. All of us have felt the hot juices of youth. Now it is our time to give sage advice."

"But who will listen? Here we are, the others will be waiting," Three Moons concluded as he scratched for admission on the side of the council lodge.

Inside the elders of four tribes had gathered. Bent Arrow marveled at this. In the old days, Kiowa and Cheyenne had been enemies. Both fought the Comanches. Now they sat as one council, along with the Apaches.

Three Moons might have been reading his mind. "Funny, the Apaches are here. Arrogant fellows. They claim that long ago, in the Grandfather Times, before the white men came, they rode all this land, even into Kansas."

Bent Arrow grunted. "It might be. My Shining People had the sacred Black Hills all to ourselves before the white man. Then came our cousins the Dakota. We fought at first, then made friends, then learned of our common home in the land of sunrise. By then, my people ranged as far as Kansas in the long summer. Our southern brothers came north to meet us. The Apaches were nowhere to be found in those days. Unnnh—Stone Calf wants to begin."

After the pipe ritual, Stone Calf of the Kiowa made a short address that laid out the purpose of the grand council. His words were not met with pleasure. Heated discussion followed.

Brave Heart, Comanche, intoned, "The whites are like a flood. They keep coming, even into this land that was supposed to be ours forever."

"It has happened before, my brother," Three Moons, Kiowa, pointed out.

"Soon not even this poor and wasted ground will be left to us," Fat Bear, Apache, stated.

"There is great discontent among the tribes shoved

so close together in such a small place," Stone Calf pointed out.

"We must not fight each other," Bent Arrow pleaded.

"No, we dare not," Three Moons supported him. "Nothing would please the white-eyes more than to see us kill each other."

"This strain between different people is not the worst matter that threatens us. Even as we speak," Stone Calf informed the elders, "angry young men are gathering to attack the bluecoat soldiers at the outpost called Camp Fenton."

"That is not all," Bent Arrow injected, with a nod toward Stone Calf. "Kiowa braves have already raided far north into Kansas. They have burned, killed, taken scalps and driven off cattle. This we cannot allow."

Murmurs of agreement went around the circle. "It must not go on," a levelheaded Comanche chief agreed. "War with the whites would get us all killed."

"You speak wisely, Black Turtle," a northern Cheyenne chief took up the pipe to talk. "Yellow Hair, the one my people called *Int-zaya* and the Arapaho named 'Son of the Morning Star,' is still remembered by the whites and many revere him. They would cry for vengeance. Our young men must be kept in check. Some from my own camp have gone out, I am ashamed to say. Our own council will punish them when they return."

"But will they?" Stone Calf asked rhetorically. "It is too late for that. These warriors are full of sap and listen to another voice, not ours. Walks Proud, a half-blood of the Kiowas, has their ears. He promises them sure victory, easy victory and lots of white blood."

49

"Then we must stop Walks Proud," Bent Arrow stated the obvious.

Stone Calf looked sadly at the assembled leaders. "That, I'm afraid, we cannot do. He is too powerful."

5

Nozzles hung suspended from the ceiling of the long, narrow room. Pullchains connected to the arms of spring-loaded valves that controlled the gravity-feed flow of water from a rank of barrels on the roof. Joey Ridgeway stepped dripping from the shower room. Small for his age, he looked more 13 than 16. He was well-muscled and remained deeply tanned from summer sun. He dried himself briskly, thinking of the days that lay ahead.

Just to get out of here! Merrill's Academy for Young Men, in San Antonio, Texas, had all the appeal to him of an outhouse pit. Oh, he liked some of the courses all right. And some of the students. Even a rare faculty member. It was being here, and nowhere else, alone and away from Winnona Parsons, away from the heady, fantastic lovemaking to which she had introduced him three years ago. Hard to believe she was a year younger than he; yet, she knew so much.

Better get away from those thoughts, he goaded himself when he looked down at his body's swift reaction. He wound his towel around his waist and went to retrieve the wicker basket that contained his clothes. What really chafed him about Merrill's,

Joey decided, was that boarding students got to leave the campus only twice a year. For the Christmas holidays and one month in summer. Somehow Rebecca had managed to wangle him an extra two weeks right before the start of the school year. Maybe it was that Indian Studies thing she had donated a lot of money to. The friendly chirp of a familiar voice cleared the fumes of his pondering.

"Is it true you're gonna spend the last two weeks before classes off on the Gulf Coast?" Tim Hartwell asked.

Joey stopped and faced his closest friend. "Reckon so, Timmy. With my stepmother."

"Aaagh! How can that be any fun?"

"You don't know my stepmother. We'll probably camp out, fish, swim, do some shooting, all sorts of things."

"Yeah, I know what you mean. Lucky dog, see ya."

"Sure. See ya later, Timmy." Really looking forward to it, Joey hurried to retrieve his clothes. By breakfast time tomorrow he would be far from this place.

Lulled by the rattle and sway of the cars, Rebecca Caldwell relaxed in the arms of Carl Blake. Only a few hours out of San Antonio, where Rebecca would leave the train, she and Carl had borrowed the conductor's small compartment for a chance at a little privacy. They had quickly discovered the tidy, folding bunk. Clothes lay in a welter on the floor and a lowering sun painted their naked bodies in red-gold hues.

"I think this is wonderful," Rebecca murmured against Carl's chest.

52

"So do I. Are you sure you won't come along with me to Galveston?"

"No, Carl. I can't. It would be hard to explain to Joey."

"Then this is truly good-bye?"

"For now, at least. Who knows? Maybe I can join you in New Orleans. It would be nice to have fun there."

"What happened there to make you dislike it so?" Carl asked.

"Another time," Rebecca evaded. "Right now there is something more important to tend to."

"What might that be?" Carl asked, sure he knew the answer.

She explained by action, her hands busy below his waist, teasing new life into his friction warmed member. He muttered surprised expressions at her persistence and apparent insatiability. She chuckled throatily and circled his hips, pulling him over onto her.

They lay like that for a while, allowing their bodies to grow accustomed to the tingling sensations contact made. Rebecca stirred first, spread her legs and groped for the large, rigid object that lay along her stomach. With amused cooperation from Carl she directed his long shaft to the warm, moist passage which welcomed it. Rising on his hands, Carl gave a short thrust.

"Aaah! Yes, more, now, more," Rebecca pleaded.

"Are you sure? We shouldn't take the time. The conductor will be wanting his room back."

"Don't talk," Rebecca panted.

"Oh, this is what you want, eh?" Carl pulled back slightly and drove more of his manly emblem into the tight canal. Rebecca quivered and pleaded for more. He gave gladly.

53

"Oh, hurry, Carl. More, more," she entreated again.

Fully encased after long minutes, Carl paused before he began a swaying hip movement that set off showers of bright spots behind Rebecca's eyes. His long, gliding pulses built toward a crescendo that he prolonged by judicious halts and slow, titillating starts. Outside the sun slid closer to the horizon.

Blissfully Rebecca and Carl added new dimensions to their fevered coupling. Each strived to give more than they received, so that they found the pinnacle in the glorious blaze of sunset and explosive climax.

"We couldn't have devised," Rebecca gasped out, "a better way to say good-bye."

A solitary sentry kept watch at Camp Fenton. Located near the border with Texas, the Indian Territory outpost served as a resting place for passing patrols, screened unauthorized whites from taking the main trail north and often provided a distribution station for Indian allotments of cattle, flour, sugar and other commodities. Nothing ever happened there.

Or so thought the lone picket as he made his rounds while his companions slept the last hour before reveille. Only the cook and his helpers were awake at this early hour of morning. The crusty old sergeant rattled an armload of wood over the expanse of his big belly as he headed for the large outdoor cooking pit.

Some prime Texas beef had strayed in their direction and so the troops were in for a special treat. Breakfast would be steak and eggs and fried potatoes. A fine largess for men bored by uneventful duty. It would, the cook hoped, help the company to forget the scorched rice pudding of the previous night. A soft, meaty smack preceded his abrupt halt.

His armload of wood fell in a clatter, accompanied by a small gasp. One hand reached for the arrow shaft that protruded from his back. A short distance away, lured by the prospect of fresh coffee, the sentry stared in horror at the terrible sight. Before he could give the alarm, he was grabbed from behind and two dark figures materialized out of the dark.

A Cheyenne warrior raised his powerful arm and plunged it downward, which buried a large Green River trade knife in the sentry's heart.

Howling wildly, bellicose Cheyenne warriors, led by Pony Nose, swarmed into the roughly formed stockade of Camp Fenton. One wing, led by Bright Shield, ran to the fire. A cook's helper shrieked in pain and terror as two braves threw him into the fire. The second assistant, a black soldier, fell to his knees, hands lifted in supplication.

"Oh, Lord, Lord, don't kill me. I done lived through my chile'hood as a slave an' joined the army to make something of m'sself," he wailed.

"It is a great mystery," one of the warriors declared, pointing to the ebony skin.

"The Spirits have touched him," another agreed.

A third reached for his hair, scalping knife at the ready. "It is like the buffalo!" he exclaimed in surprise.

Bright Shield appeared to one side. He listened to their impressions of the black soldier and shouted for all to hear, "No man is to touch this one. He is beloved of the Spirits."

Released at once, the black soldier slumped to the ground. He didn't know what the words meant, only that he had so far been spared. Maybe his momma had been right, he reasoned. He might have a real

55

important reason to be glad he was black.

Around him, white troops did not fare so well. Men screamed and died on their cots, others rushed forth to be felled by arrows and bullets. Tent cloth tore and flapped in a rising dawn breeze. Before long flames crackled in the canvas and provided light. Both sides seized its advantage to aid in the killing of one another.

"Stand fast! Form a skirmish line," the young officer in command yelled, his voice cracking like it had in his youth.

"You men, open fire," a frantic sergeant bellowed. He turned part way and clubbed a Cheyenne into the dirt with the butt of his Springfield. Two arrows moaned their eerie song before they thudded into his chest.

More Cheyenne warriors swarmed into the compound. Flames now spouted from the shattered windows of the log headquarters. The besieged young company commander had drawn his surviving troopers into a tight defensive ring behind an improvised breastwork of dead horses and men. War whoops rang in the predawn air. They sounded gleeful and victorious to the lieutenant. He raised up to fire at a brave painted entirely in vertical halves of black and white. The hammer of his Colt fell on an expended primer.

Instantly he dropped his revolver and snatched up a Springfield from a dead trooper beside him. No time! No time! His mind screamed the warning at him as he checked the chamber for a round. He looked up in time to see the domino warrior towering over him with a wicked looking war club. Blindly he thrust forward with the Springfield.

A hideous shriek rewarded his efforts and the weapon thrashed wildly in his grip. Silently he gave

56

thanks to the forethought of the deceased soldier who had followed standing orders and put his bayonet on the rifle. His gratitude lasted only a moment before the world exploded in brightness as a .56 caliber slug from an old Spencer pulped his brain.

By then even the slender blackjack pine poles that formed the palisade burned brightly. One by one the white soldiers fell to the relentless fury of the Cheyenne Dog Soldiers. The warrior society had been kept alive in secret, binding new members to it with the forbidden hope of a return to the old ways. Now it paid dividends for Pony Nose. When the last trooper died, the scalping began in earnest.

All of the rampart except the area around the main gate had been engulfed in flame when Pony Nose gave the order to leave. "To your ponies, quickly. Leave this place," he shouted over and over.

Quickly the Cheyenne obeyed him. Mounted again, they rode off into the breaking day. They left behind nothing but burning ruin and broken, mutilated corpses.

He looked like a forlorn waif, standing by himself, away from the other clots of people waiting to meet arrivals or board the train. Yet he stood ramrod straight, more a miniature man than a boy. Rebecca's heart knew a mother's pain and pride at the sight. Joey, poor Joey, she thought watching from the window of her Pullman car. He hadn't grown more than an inch nor put on a pound since she had last seen him.

She had cause to know that puberty had been well entrenched in the towheaded little lad. Yet, for some mysterious reason, all other areas of development had been arrested. Except for his mind, she

57

amended, which had always been keen, curious and active. Brains and balls, a coarser part of her nature mocked her. No, she couldn't think of Joey that way. He was all she had left of Grover Ridgeway and a year of fabulous peace on the high plains ranch. She gathered her things and started from the car, a porter in her wake with a large carpetbag.

"Joey," she called to him as she alighted on the platform.

"Rebecca," he responded, the frown dissolving on his high, smooth forehead. "Mom," he appended in a tone of genuine pleasure. "I began to worry you weren't on this train."

"I'm here, all right. We have to see to getting *Sila* out of the stock car and then we can go shopping."

Joey frowned, his slight frame still in the adult pose she had first witnessed. "What kind of shopping?"

"A tent, camping gear, maybe a canoe or small boat," she ticked off.

Beaming, Joey almost clapped his hands in childish pleasure, then caught himself and resumed his recently infused reserve. "That's—that's wonderful. We are really going to live out along the shore?"

"I thought so. Maybe even find a small island all to ourselves. Would you like that?"

"Uh-huh. Anything'd be better than that dormitory."

It was Rebecca's turn to frown. "You don't like the school?"

"Oh, school's all right," Joey said offhandedly. "It's havin' to live there that bothers me. All those *boys* around, sleeping beside you, above you, everywhere," he ended miserably.

Rebecca tried for lightness. "I suppose as an almost married man that could cramp your style a little. How about the others? Do they feel the same?"

"Ha! Most of them *like* it. Only a few of the upperclassmen know anything at all about girls." His reserve broke and Joey looked down at his shoes. "And they call me 'Squirt' and 'Shrimp.' "

Fighting the desire to laugh, Rebecca commiserated with her stepson. "I must say you've impressed me with your grown-up manners and excellent taste in clothes. How are your grades?"

"Okay," he answered quietly. "Mrs. Parsons picked my suit, and we have a class in what they call 'deportment' at the academy," he explained away his little man demeanor.

"What say we tend to *Sila* and start that shopping?" Rebecca prodded.

Twenty minutes later Rebecca and Joey stalked the outfitters shops on Alamo Plaza. Every imaginable item of frontier equipage could be purchased for a price. The variety of choices, rather than availability, made selecting a suitable tent difficult. Through the forenoon hours Rebecca concentrated on the task extremely conscious of how important this expedition would be to Joey.

"Why don't we stop for lunch?" she suggested after leaving the fourth shop without making a single purchase.

"That's fine." Joey sounded listless Rebecca noticed with concern.

"Then pick a place," she suggested, then added, "I've been thinking. When we get to the Parsons' place to get your pony, we might ask if Winnona could come along?"

Joey brightened in an instant, eyes sparkling, face animated. "That would be great! Perfect." Impulsively he grabbed her and hugged her tightly. "This is going to be a fantastic trip."

Although traveling in the opposite direction of their intended course, the short journey to the Parsons' ranch turned out to be a pleasant one. Rebecca and Joey became more relaxed in the company of each other. They had left the newly purchased gear in storage at a reliable warehouse owned by a friend of the Russel family. Her brief visit with Simon Asher had opened old wounds, the scars of which she carried on her heart.

Poor, dear Bob Russel, murdered three years ago by Chris Starret. So far his death had gone unavenged. Grief over the lost love turned to anger and Rebecca finished the arrangements without revealing the depth of her feelings. She hadn't hidden it from Joey, however, and his slender young arms around her neck that night and soft words of consolation helped a great deal in breaking down barriers. It made the hours of the day-and-a-half journey go by swiftly.

At the Parsons' homestead they found Amanda Parsons working a field and Winnona nursing her younger brothers, Billy and Tommy, both of whom had come down with the frightful and sometimes fatal disease of measles. Rebecca had seen the terrible waste brought to Sioux villages by the white man's disease and she knew of every means used to treat the illness.

Winnona had followed some excellent advice, Rebecca allowed. Both boys remained in bed, their eyes covered by damp cloths, their naked bodies frequently bathed with cool wellwater. Much to Rebecca's relief and approval, Winnona burned the scraps of old bed sheets she used. It created a rather awk-ward situation when Joey made a quiet revelation.

"I've never had measles," he said, on the verge of pouting.

Nor had she, Rebecca realized. Which put them in the barn over night. They left early the next morn-ing, without Winnona and hopefully not infected. Joey tried to put a cheerful face on the matter.

"It's all right, Mom. I—I can get along okay with-out Winnona along. Although it sure would have been fun."

Rebecca sighed with relief. "Thank you, Joey. I'm glad to see you'll not let this put a shadow over our whole trip to the Gulf."

"Oh, no. I want to eat shrimp until I bust, have oysters and all those things. Peddlers sell them in the streets outside the academy, but we never have them and we aren't permitted to buy from the street mer-chants."

Light laughter accentuated Rebecca's relieved re-ply. "I guarantee you that we'll have all the shrimp and oysters, and anything else you want, until they run out of our ears."

Joey squinched his face into a sour expression as his active imagination created an image of her words. Then his high-pitched giggle brightened the day. "Yeah, well, I sure hope this is the only trouble we have."

"I can't think of any possible thing that might bring us trouble," Rebecca responded in lighthearted disregard of Fate.

6

Two "Tall Hat" Delaware men reached Ft. Sill in late morning. They walked beside their two-wheel cart of trade goods. One of them occasionally applied a limber willow switch to the haunches of the mule that drew the high-sided vehicle. They both took note of the unusual number of crows that flew about or roosted in the sparse cottonwood trees.

"That is a bad sign," Charlie One Horse remarked to his companion.

Skokie Middleton, a true half-breed, rather than by white circumlocution, snorted, "Are you going superstitious again, Charlie?"

"No. But if I was a Kiowa or a Cheyenne or a Comanche, I'd think twice about going out on a day with that many crows flocked around."

An hour's travel brought them to the big parade ground. They crossed it diagonally to the sandstone and clapboard headquarters building. Charlie halted the cart and they approached the trio of steps that led to the full-length, roofed porch. The two sentries stopped them.

"State your name and your business, Injun," one young trooper sneered.

"I'm Charlie One Horse. We're Delaware traders and . . ."

"You got nothin' we want to trade for," the rude sentry interrupted.

"We have bad news for General Britton."

"I'll bet you do."

"It is important that I see General Britton," Charlie persisted patiently.

"You tell me all about it, 'cause the Gen'ral's in a staff meeting."

"I'll tell the general, and no one else," Charlie bristled.

"You keep that attitude an' I'll call the Provost Sergeant and have you stockaded."

"What's going on here, Trooper?" Brigade Sergeant Major Brandon Doyle demanded from the doorway. His red hair was only half contained under his kepi and his auburn mustache flowed in the morning breeze. "Hey, Charlie One Horse, what brings you to Fort Sill?"

"Sergeant Doyle, it is a bad thing. I must talk to the general. Camp Fenton is—it is all gone."

"What do you mean, Charlie?" Doyle demanded.

"I will tell all to you when I see General Britton," Charlie declared stubbornly.

"C'mon in, then. The staff meetin's just breaking up," Doyle invited.

"Beggin' your pardon, Sergeant," the trooper blurted, "but Col. Trask won't like it you lettin' these dirty Injuns into headquarters."

Charlie One Horse fixed the soldier with a cold eye. "Tell me one thing, soldier. Do you speak any language besides English?"

"What's that got—? Naw. English is good enough for anything."

"I beg to differ. We 'dirty Injuns,' on the other

hand, are from one of the five civilized tribes. We speak our own tongue, Delaware, also Cherokee, Algonquin, Lakota and Cheyenne. English, as well, as you can tell. And I dare say we speak it considerably better than you do. Now, if you will step aside and let us enter, we promise not to tell my good friend General Britton how discourteous you've been to us."

"Charlie, Charlie, you're a pistol," Doyle declared through a chuckle. Catching sight of the brigade adjutant in the orderly room, the sergeant major hailed him. "Col. Trask, there's two Delawares here to see the general, sir."

"Charlie One Horse is one of them, I'll wager," Trask said affably. "Bring them on in."

From outside, Charlie heard the sentry who had remained silent admonishing his snotty companion. "Boy, you really put your foot in it that time. That Indian's a friend of Doyles *and* old brass-ass Trask. Not to mention Lieutenant General Albert Britton."

It took considerable effort for Charlie to keep his broad, nutmeg face from dissolving into merriment. He hurried along beside BSM Doyle, three feet behind Col. Trask, into the general's office. Lt. Gen. Britton shook hands with Charlie and his new partner.

"This is a bad day, General," Charlie began. "This is my new partner, Skokie Middleton. We came by way of Camp Fenton, two days ago."

"Charlie, do I have to get a spade and dig it out of you?" Britton asked.

"They're all dead, General. All except one black fellow, he's buryin' the rest. Everything's burned down. Nothing but hot coals and ashes where the camp was."

Lt. Gen. Britton paled considerably. "A black soldier?"

"Yes, sir," Col. Trask injected. "That would be Amos Dibble, a cook's helper. Said he didn't want to serve with a black unit, wanted to prove himself on his own. I'll get a detail ready to ride to Fenton."

"Yes, do that," the general said absently. "Charlie, why'd they spare him?"

"Superstition, General," Charlie answered candidly. "It was Cheyennes who did it. We found lots of red painted arrow shafts. They and the Dakota, Crow, consider a man with black skin to be touched by the Spirits. Bad medicine to kill them."

"I've heard of that," Gen. Britton mused. "Horace, call the staff back here and the regimental commanders as well. I want them to hear Charlie's story. Then we'll take to the field."

"About time, I'd say," Trask muttered. "Right away, sir. Sergeant Major, see to assembling the officers and pick a detail for burial duty at Camp Fenton."

"Yes, sir, right away, sir." Doyle started for the door. "Trumpeter," he bawled, "sound Officers' Call."

Intchi-Dijin watched the people below. His heart was heavy. The dark feelings inside him matched the gullied face that was more fright mask than human features. Heavily muscled forearms folded across his barrel chest, he took in the wretched hovels his people were constrained to live in here at Fort Sill. Few had the look of a true *wickiup*. Most were mere brush arbors, while some dwellings were made of the white man's canvas.

This was not the way for the *Tloh-ka-dih-nadidah-hae* to live. The "Rise from the Grass" people had always been free and proud. Even before the removal to Fort Sill from the San Carlos reservation many among the people had taken to using the White Mountain name for the people, *Tindé. Intchi-Dijin*—Black Wind—rejected that. It sounded too much like the hated sheep raiser Navajo, who called themselves the *Diné*. Black Wind turned from the scene to address the two young companions who squatted to either side of him.

"What are your thoughts, *Wano-boono?*"

Calico Turkey blinked and ran a wide hand over his broad face. "He speaks with words of power."

"And you, *Ne-pot-on-je?*" *Intchi-Dijin* queried.

"It is said his medicine is strong," the smooth faced Bear Watcher responded.

Black Wind snorted. "I do not believe that his words or his medicine will make us safe from the white men's bullets," Black Wind rumbled. "We have heard tales of that from when we were on our mothers' hips. Only Iron Shirt of the Comanche ever proved that in battle. And only for himself, and only until the white men came out with cartridge rifles. The iron shirt of the *españols* was proof against muzzle loaded charges. Bullets from the Sharps, Spencer, and Henry punched holes through it like through cooked fat. All the same," he went on, "our people languish here and die. We are no longer free.

"Not to be free steals one's pride. I will ride with Walks Proud."

"And I," Bear Watcher declared.

"Count on me, too," Calico Turkey agreed.

"Among us, we control how many warriors?" Black Wind asked, growing excited.

"I have sworn to me two hands," *Ne-pot-on-je* stated.

"And I one hand and three," *Wano-boono* added.

"With my two hands and two, that makes three two hands and three (33) *Tloh-ka-dih-nadidah-hae* to bring to Walks Proud. We will gather our men and ride in the morning to join Walks Proud."

Charlie One Horse went over every detail of what he knew of the raid on Camp Fenton. The staff officers and regimental commanders listened with tight interest. Through it all, one man seemed most agitated. Colonel Lydell Simms sat on the edge of his chair, back rigidly erect, though he gave the impression of squirming in impatience.

Well known as a fire-eater in the tradition of Custer and Sheridan, Lydell Simms had twice been passed over for general due to his often punitive methods of dealing with Indians. Even the War Department had a gag point. Now Simms saw this as vindication of his point of view. At last Lt. Gen. Britton made a summary of the situation and opened the conference for discussion.

"I'll entertain any suggested plans of action," he said quietly.

Col. Lydell Simms raised his hand first. "The Cheyenne have to be punished. The entire brigade should participate. I propose that we sweep down on the Cheyenne and dispose of every one of them, man, woman, child, dog and pony."

"Why, that's preposterous, Lydell," Col. Horace Trask exploded. "The United States Army does not make war on women and children."

"Custer did," Simms snapped. "At the Washita, remember? And he was following official policy. Sheridan said it, 'Nits make lice.' If we make an object lesson of the Cheyenne, exterminate them entirely, the others will think twice about any uprising."

"You are wrong," Lt. Gen. Britton stated flatly. "Our problem is not with the usual leaders. The councils all argue for peace. It's the young men and this Red Messiah they're listening to. Walks Proud. A Kiowa half-breed who's real name is Simon Blackthorne. He was educated in the East and has a lifelong hatred for all whites. He is also a powerful, hypnotic speaker who can sway nearly anyone to his cause. If you want to hunt down someone, Lydell, go after him. In fact, I'm making that an order. Here's how we're going to do it.

"We'll use the entire brigade, as you suggested," Gen. Britton outlined. "Regimental commanders, I want a patrol schedule from each of you by Retreat Formation this afternoon. We'll make sweeps to every point of the compass, simultaneously and in such a manner to give each company time off for rest and necessary repair of equipment. The object is to locate and apprehend Walks Proud. We'll bring him here, try him and hang him. Those captured with him will be held in the stockade, pending a peaceful solution after he has been removed from a position of influence. If there are no questions at this time, you are dismissed until five minutes after Retreat."

So far the recreation trip had gone quite well. Rebecca Caldwell and Joey Ridgeway had ridden along the coast from Galveston until they spotted a small island that appealed to them. A local ferryman had taken them over for a nominal fee. They set up camp, using a 12x14x8 foot outside pole wall tent with awnings and privacy curtain as the central feature. That stored supplies and fodder for the horses, while a 16', buffalo hide lodge served for sleeping and social activities. The plains tipi looked out of place on a Texas Gulf island.

That didn't bother its occupants. Rebecca wore

her most favored costume, a doeskin dress, with simple bead and quill decorations, and colorful Sioux moccasins. Joey wore only a loincloth and moccasins, once in a while adding his hair-pipe breast plate to ornaments of choker, bracelet and anklet. The boy's complaints about Merrill's Academy ceased on the second day at the island.

Now, on the third morning, as they watched the clouds turn from pink to white and sea birds skim over the small wavelets of the cove, Joey came to Rebecca and gave her a big hug.

"That was a great breakfast," he said quietly. "I feel stuffed."

"No wonder. You ate four fish and five pieces of fry bread. Next thing, you'll be getting fat."

For a moment, the disappointment returned. "I can't even grow, let alone get fat." Joey's lower lip slid out in a pink pout.

Such agonies to growing up, Rebecca thought in a moment of distress. Although entirely different in nature, her own travails had seemed larger than life until she fell in love with Four Horns. Sighing, she tried to remove the slight frown from her forehead before exploring the subject.

"Joey, I've told you before that people grow up, mature at different rates. We have no control over our bodies in that respect."

"Yeah, but . . . Billy Parsons is as big as I am and he's only thirteen."

An idea formed. "And Billy is still a little boy, right? Do you remember when we lived in the Oglala village? One very necessary event in your life that had to have happened before you could take your dreaming time and find your secret name?"

Joey considered a moment, brightened. "Sure. I had to be able to—ah—well, you know," he concluded weakly, face crimson. "The *pezuta* made us show him that we could before we were taken for the *inipi* and then sent from the sweat lodge ceremony to find our place to fast and pray and dream. And— and, you're right, Billy can't do that. So he's slow in growing in some ways, too." A blissful expression bloomed on Joey's face and he hugged Rebecca tightly, slipping into his native tongue entirely.

"Pila maya ina, tecik hila."

"And I love you, *micinksi,*" Rebecca answered huskily.

"Thank you, mother," he said again in English. Then, gathering his school learned reserve, he asked, "What shall we do today?"

"By the time we clean up after breakfast it will be too late to fish until near sundown. So I thought we might spend some time exploring the island this morning."

An impish grin lighted Joey's face. "I sorta favor swimming."

"We can do both. We'll explore and then when we come back all hot, sweaty, and dusty, we can swim to clean off, then have a late lunch."

"You've thought of everything," Joey charged.

"Not everything. While we're here we can let things happen as they develop. That's bound to appeal, doesn't it?"

"Sure. All right, you get the dishes done and I'll saddle the horses," Joey directed.

"Just a minute, young man. You help clean up first. Do you want to wash or dry?"

"Damnation!" Joey expelled under his breath. "Washing dishes is women's work."

"Not in this camp. Not if the only man wants to have his meals cooked for him."

"Aw, Mom," Joey bemoaned his fate, though

70

he went off to scrub the cast-iron skillet with sand.

Their exploration extended beyond noon. They located several shacks and a number of lean-tos, obviously the work of locals from the Texas mainland, who used them for fishing or hunting trips. One was fairly well made, of small logs, chinked with crushed oyster and clam shells and plaster. It showed signs of recent occupation. Hot and dirty, their skins glistening with moisture, Rebecca and Joey returned to their camp at the cove more than ready for the cooling waters of the Gulf of Mexico.

"Don't forget a bar of soap," Rebecca reminded as she pulled off her doeskin dress.

Rebecca Caldwell had grown up somewhat wild by civilized standards, had lived and played much of her childhood alone. She never developed the body taboos of her white relations, splashing around in the water of the creek on the Caldwell homestead in the buff and thinking nothing of it. Only when around adult whites, particularly her uncles Virgil and Ezekial, did her mother insist she go completely clothed, even to hateful shoes.

For his part, Joey had lived on an isolated ranch, much removed from civilized codes as had his stepmother. He and his brother, and their friends bathed in stock tanks and swam naked together in the rivers of the high plains. Their lives among the Sioux, mother and son, had done little to instill body consciousness taboos either. So they saw nothing objectionable to strip on the strand and leave their clothes behind as they entered the water.

After a thorough bath, to remove trail and forest stains, they frolicked for half an hour in idyllic splendor. Sunlight reflecting off the water limited their range of vision. Joey began diving to the sandy bottom, the water so clear he could pick his targets

71

from the surface. After one particularly long dive he surfaced with a shout of triumph.

"Look at this!" He waved a strap of metal, nails studding it, with rotted wood clinging to some of them.

Rebecca swam over to him and tread water. "What do you think it is?"

"I—I don't know," Joey admitted, the rusty object held close to the surface. "Could be off some sort of chest." He brightened, excited even more. "Maybe it's pirate treasure."

"Oh, don't go getting worked up over something like that. More likely some fishing boat that got caught in a storm."

"I'm going to dive again and find out." With that, Joey upended and made a clean surface dive. It left Rebecca holding the unidentified artifact.

Through the wave distortion of the water, she watched her stepson search the white sand bottom. He wriggled and kicked, drove upward for a long gasp of air and went down again. His hands raised clouds of sand that obscured what he was doing. He stopped abruptly and lifted something. Flexing his knees he drove for the surface.

It took two tries and he nearly lost his latest find before his straw white hair broke through the waves. "It's a bell. A ship's bell," he shouted excitedly. The weight dragged at him, threatening to sink him in the depths.

"Let's get a little closer in," Rebecca suggested.

"I don't want to lose this place."

"We should have brought the boat."

Their camp gear included a small canoe and paddles, which they used the previous day to obtain the fish that had been supper and breakfast. Joey thought on it. His nose slipped

72

below the next wavelet before he spoke.

"You take the bell and go for the boat, huh? I'll dive again. Just think, maybe there *is* pirate treasure."

Distracted by Joey's find, their backs to the outlet of the cove, they failed to notice a handsome scooner sail into the small bay. Tall sails to the wind, the sleek, all teak boat glided across the water. Its brass brightwork glittered in the sunlight. Within a hundred yards of them now, the vessel slid serenely past.

A tall figure appeared above the combing of the cockpit, and the mainsail luffed as it dropped. Quickly he gathered it in and secured it, then returned to the tiller, speed reduced with only the jib and foresail drawing.

Forty-two feet of luxurious boat grew closer to them as it passed behind, headed for the deepwater portion of the cove, close to shore. Unaware, Rebecca sought to get Joey to agree to swim in with her, sharing the weight of the bell, then return for another dive. A loud splash drew her attention to the visitor as the sailor cast the anchor over the side.

Startled, Rebecca and Joey waved with free hands. "Get away," Rebecca warned. "We're right here in the water. Steer away from us!"

He saw their bobbing heads then and gave a jaunty wave in return. With a light step, he gained the foredeck with a shiny brass tube in one hand. This he extended to reveal a telescope. With careful swipes, he directed the front lens toward them.

Sudden enlightenment hit Joey. "Hey, he can see us. I mean—below the water see us."

Rebecca let out a whoop and started desperately for the shore. Joey joined her a second later, floundering with the heavy bell. Forced to abandon it, his bare, pale white buttocks flashed wetly in the sun before he smoothed out into a respectable crawl. When she could touch bottom, Rebecca braced herself and waved off the boat.

"Hey, you, go away. Get out of here. We—we don't have anything on."

Faint laughter answered her and she squinted to see the man at work on the foresail, which he now lowered and furled, securing it like the mainsail with gaskets. Fuming, Rebecca and Joey crouched in the shallows.

"Damn him," Joey complained. "I had to drop the bell."

"How are we going to get dressed with that—that Peeping Tom out there?" Rebecca spoke to the most immediate problem.

"Oh, to hell with him," Joey replied. "He won't see anything he hasn't seen before." So saying, he rose and walked unhurriedly to shore.

On the strand he retrieved Rebecca's dress and carried it out to her. She turned her back and slipped it on. By then their unwelcome visitor had the jib secured. Walking with what dignity she could muster, in a wet doeskin dress, she left the water and headed for the shelter of the wall tent. Joey slowly dressed in full view of the boat, his posture one of defiance. Let him look, he seemed to imply.

"Rebecca—Mom, look now," Joey cried suddenly. "He's letting down a little boat."

In minutes the dinghy headed for the beach. The man, rowing with his back to them, took on a puzzlingly familiar appearance to Rebecca as he drew nearer. When the prow scraped into the sand, he climbed over the side and drew the dinghy up on the sand. He turned with a friendly wave and a big smile.

"Becky, hello. I thought I'd find you around one

74

of these islands," Carlton Blake called happily.

"Carlton Blake, I could happily break your neck right now," Rebecca growled as he approached.

7

Carlton Blake introduced himself to Joey and invited the two surprised people to have a late dinner aboard his boat. The forty-two footer carried a crew of three; one deckhand, a majordomo of sorts, and a cook. Carl rowed ashore in the lingering twilight and brought his guests to the deck of the *Ulysses*.

"Named for the famous hero of the *Odyssey*," he explained, "not our former president."

Joey, who had been reading Homer at the academy, brightened. "Have you met the Gorgons yet? Or run into the Cyclops?"

"Nothing quite so exciting, Sonny," Carl replied, only a slight bit condescending. Joey winced and Carl astutely picked up on it. "Sorry. I can't imagine that childish name being applied to anyone who reads Homer. Is your school using the original Greek, Joe?"

"N-no, sir. It's the Oxford translation."

"And a very good one, let me assure you. Without it I would never have made it through the Greek text when I was at Oxford."

Joey's eyes grew round. "You went to Oxford?"

"I certainly wouldn't go to Cambridge. Sorry, that's a very English joke. The schools' rivalries and all. Tell me, how have you two been enjoying your stay?"

"Fine," Rebecca replied, then added in mock crossness, "until a nosey young man put his spyglass on us while we were swimming."

"Well put, though as I recall, that swimming party was quite raw."

"Carl," Rebecca squeaked.

"All past and done with. When I sail out of here you can go back to your—ah—usual routine. Truth to tell, I've always believed that to be the only proper, natural way to swim. Now, would you object to a little wine before supper? A small glass for the young man, too?"

"I—ah—I suppose that would be all right, this being a special occasion," Rebecca agreed.

Joey looked as though he would burst. Being treated like an adult. It exceeded his wildest imaginings. He accepted the stemmed glass gravely and sipped sparingly. It teased his tongue and burned his throat. Not at all like beer. He tried another swallow. Then the stiff, formal, gray-haired majordomo appeared to announce dinner in what he called the "main salon."

No effort had been spared. Elegant silver service, translucent china, damask lace table napery, and an array of savory, appetizing dishes, many of which Rebecca could not identify. Taken in small amounts they all tasted divine. More wine came with dinner. Afterward, Rebecca took a rich, ruby port and Carl brandy.

Carl lit a cigar and Joey longed to be away in some secret place so he could roll one of the forbidden cigarettes to which he and the other boys at the Merrill Academy subscribed with utter dedication. The conversational lull swung into new life with adult talk that soon bored Joey. Excusing himself he went onto the foredeck, stripped out of his "civilized" clothes Rebecca had insisted he wear, rolled them in a tight cylinder, which he put in an oilcloth pouch and dived over the side.

With sure, powerful strokes he swam to shore. He let the balmy night air dry him, then dressed in loincloth and moccasins and lighted a fire. Surprisingly he found his thoughts straying to Carlton Blake. A smile curved Joey's full, sensuous lips as he discovered he had come to like the intruder. Back on *Ulysses*, talk had grown quieter and more intimate.

Their chores completed by ten o'clock, the crew turned in. Carl and Rebecca sat in the comfortable, padded curve of the pilot's seat in the cockpit. A brilliant frosting of stars shone above them. Far to the east the moon made a yellow glow as it began to rise. Carl put an arm around Rebecca's shoulder.

"It would make my aspirations complete if you would spend the night aboard."

"Oh, Carl, I would love that. But there is Joey and . . ."

"At least part of the night?" he suggested. "Martin and Minny have gone to bed, so has Trent. Have you . . . have you ever made love on the deck of a boat at anchor under the stars?"

"No, I—Carl, you have me at a terrible disadvantage. I—I—yes, yes, I'll stay a while."

Carl kissed her then, long and hard. Swiftly her ardor grew from a tiny, gnawing awareness to a raging desire. Rebecca's heart pounded and her vision blurred. She clung to him while Carl undressed her. Not a word or act of protest came as he slid her out of the filmy black dress and laid bare her most bounteous bosom. His lips found her breasts and fluttered over them, fairy wings that fed her growing passion.

Her own hands and lips busy, Rebecca opened Carl's shirt and ran a flat palm over his smooth, hairless skin. She worked lower, to his waist, undid his belt. His trousers came off with little effort and she stood to let her dress fall. They embraced again.

78

"Carl — Carl — I dreamed of you. I couldn't bear giving up your magnificent body forever. You said you would sail among the islands. I hoped, planned, waited for the off chance you would find where we camped." Rebecca groaned, nearly bent double with the intensity of her desire. "Take me, oh, take me now."

Carl eased Rebecca back on the padded bench and worked his way between her silken thighs. With the same teasing gravity with which he had pierced her before, he slowly inserted his pulsing member. Impaled on his heated manhood, Rebecca's thoughts whirled away. She flexed and raised her hips, greedy for more.

Conscious of the need for discreet silence, Carl suppressed his own euphoric sensations as he drove deeply into her. A fierceness of ardor came upon him and the boat, large as it was, began to undulate to each thrust. Rebecca bit her lip and squeezed her lids tightly shut. Then she opened them to a splendorous new beauty as he managed a full-length thrust that pistoned in the slippery, elastically clinging passage that tingled to the pandemonium created by his friction.

Shivering they clung to each other, driven into a private world of unending marvels. Rebecca saw the stars, heard strange music and spun into the sweet moment of oblivion not once or twice, but four times before she became conscious of Carl's roughened breath, his erratic rhythm and the massive, trembling arrival of his completion.

"Oh, my, it is every bit as good, as wonderful as I remember. But did you know the stars remained in their places? None fell. I'm surprised. I was sure they would."

"We can try again, see if we can shake them from their courses," Carl suggested, reaching for her.

"Is there time? I really should be back before midnight," Rebecca cautioned.

79

Carl rose and consulted the binnacle clock. "There's plenty, if we hurry."

"Who wants to hurry. Make it long, make it last forever," Rebecca pleaded as she reached for his magnificent organ, already semi-erect and growing to the occasion.

Far off from the eyes and ears of the soldiers, in the place where the whites would least expect it, right there on the Ft. Sill reservation, the drums throbbed and fires flickered. The victorious Kiowa and Cheyenne warriors danced their triumph and displayed the scalps taken. Walks Proud and his principal advisors stood slightly apart from the dance ground, watching with impassive faces, arms folded in five-point Hudson's Bay blankets that draped their bodies from shoulder to knee.

"Let them tire a little, then I will speak," Walks Proud told his counselors. "We have all night."

An hour later clearly half of the dancers had dropped out. Walks Proud stepped before the largest fire and raised both arms above his head. The colorful blanket slid from his body and settled on the grass. "My brothers, this is a good day for the Kiowa, the Cheyenne, the Comanche. These proud men have tasted white man's blood. They have killed, burned, created fear and confusion. All is as it should be." His voice changed pitch, became grave.

"But I must tell you that it will not remain so unless we all abandon everything that is white in our lives. No more whiskey. No more white man's sugar or coffee, no more stinking meat or sand-filled cornmeal, no flour-that-moves. We do not eat bugs, we do not eat worms. Let the white man choke on his tainted food. Live by the old ways and I promise you that you will be able to shed the whites' bullets like raindrops."

Loud whoops and yips answered him. The drum throbbed a swift, short beat and fell silent. Eyes bright with expectation, the warriors gathered closer around Walks Proud as a shower of sparks ascended into the velvety darkness.

"We have only begun. The white man has had but a taste of our vengeance. Our next raid will be against the whiskey peddlers in a white settlement not far off in the Nations. We can ride there, destroy the white demon liquor and be back in the same day."

They loved it. Frenzied dancing began again. Warriors who had not pledged themselves to the Red Messiah's crusade in the past rushed forward to touch the war pipe in symbolic gesture of their allegiance. Through it all, Walks Proud looked on with cruel, cynical yellow eyes.

On the third night since Carlton Blake came to the cove, Joey Ridgeway remained ashore by his choice. "Three's company," he said lightly to Rebecca Caldwell, with a wink.

He knew full well what went on out on the sloop. From his own limited experience with Winnona Parsons, Joey knew that fresh glow that a woman has the next morning. It aroused him agonizingly. He had thought staying behind would ease some of the pressure. He found he was wrong.

Images of two naked people in a spacious bed, their bodies coupled and thrusting together in splendor clawed at him. He longed for the comfort of Winnona's luscious figure and perfectly fitted contours. Before he could divert himself he discovered he had achieved a large, painful erection. He knew greater misery. Joey tried to free his mind, think of other things.

Steamy images rose instead. All hot and slick and silky smooth. Wonderful, thrilling friction of sliding back and forth, on and on. Soft moans and little cries of delight, a slender, agile body supported above his own, buttocks churning around and around, grinding deeper, deeper. With a gasp Joey threw off his loincloth and sprinted into the water.

It didn't work like the cold showers of the academy. He found no relief. A half dozen rapid laps along the beach did no good either. Dripping and still in an agony of arousal, he came from the water. His urges had become so intense that he suddenly discovered his hand straying to his groin. Some terrible imp inside him clamored for him to "Go on, do it!"

For a long, frozen moment, Joey warred with himself. Then all resistance melted and he found himself ready to settle for what he considered silly kid stuff. That childish substitute for the reality he so desperately wanted. With fingers closing around his rigid staff, he went stone still at a loud rustle in the screen of brush beyond the beach.

Quickly he located his loincloth and covered his turgid organ. A couple of musical titters sounded closer and then more rattling of the bush. Joey withdrew silently into shadow and watched intently at the point where he expected to see something, or someone emerge onto the beach.

Out came two figures. Lovely, leggy, shapely, female, and *very naked*. Joey's jaw dropped and he stared in fascination as the sweet vision moved across the grassy strip and onto the sand at the water's edge. The moon came from behind a cloud and Joey made a startling discovery. The girls were identical twins. At least from this distance they seemed to be.

Long, black hair swaying, they wriggled as though caressed by moonbeams. Their delicious, ripe bodies produced such maddening desire that Joey groaned aloud. Instantly the girls turned toward the sound. Startled by his outburst, and their reaction, Joey sought to squeeze himself further back in the underbrush. The two naked beauties exchanged some unheard comments and started toward him.

"There's someone around here, Judy, I know it."

"You're right, Jenner, I heard it too."

"We'll find 'em," Judy declared confidently.

"You bet we will," her twin agreed.

It took only three minutes. Giggling and tugging on Joey's arms, the girls brought him out on the strand. Their voices were rich in the local accent.

"C'mon, Injun boy, join us in a little bare swim," Judy urged.

"Shoot, ain't nobody gonna find us, 'cept you," Jennifer admonished. "Judy's right, you look like an Injun in that getup. Come on, let's get it off you."

"I—I don't even know you," Joey protested. Worries over how he could explain this to Rebecca swam in his head. Worse thoughts of what Winnona would say plagued him.

"That's easy. I'm Judith Fouchet and this is my sister, Jennifer."

"Pleased to meet you," Jennifer added.

"I—ah—I—er, that is . . ."

"Ain't you got a name?" Judy asked.

For all his concern about this compromising situation, Joey could not take his eyes off their heavenly bodies. He figured them to be a year, maybe two, younger than himself, with small, firm, pert breasts, pink and upthrust. They curved nicely and had flaring hip bones. Identical little swirls marked their navels, above thin, wispy strands of ebony hair—fuzz really— that did little to conceal the dark lines of their clefts.

"Ah—Jo—Joey Ridgeway," Joey responded shakily.

Jennifer was no longer holding his wrist. She ran [a] soft, warm hand over his shoulders and across h[is] chest.

"Right, then, Joey, let's get that thing off you an[d] into the water," she murmured while her sister reache[d] for the bulge in Joey's loincloth.

Joey recoiled from the intimate contact and groane[d] as though in terrible agony as Judith pulled on th[e] edge of the skimpy garment. It came away with littl[e] effort, revealing his raging erection. Both gir[ls] squealed in delight. Jennifer dropped to her knees an[d] removed his moccasins, despite his efforts to preven[t] it. Then, before she stood, she delivered a quick, w[et] kiss to the tip of his throbbing organ.

For a moment Joey thought he would pass out fro[m] the delightful sensation of Jennifer's lips on his h[ot] manhood. He let himself be tugged along to the wate[r] and into the cove. The twins proved to be good swim[-] mers. All three cut through the water energetically f[or] some twenty minutes, during which Joey's inhibition[s] dissolved and washed away. Aroused beyond an[y] pledge to be faithful to Winnona, Joey was easily le[d] to the sandy beach.

"Now, Joey, you lovely, lovely boy, we're going t[o] take you to our lair and love you until you cry f[or] mercy," Judy told him, her big, haunting, startlingl[y] blue eyes, under flairing brows, fixed on his.

"Wait a minute. I . . ." Jennifer wrapped th[e] supple fingers of her other hand around Joey[']s protruding organ and squeezed in a delightf[ul] manner. His protests dried up and he gulped, "Whe[re] is this place?"

"Off a ways in the trees," Judy informed him. "Ou[r] family built it for a place to get away once in a whil[e.] We come over in our pirogue to get away from th[e] skeeters. Funny, but there ain't any on the islan[d]

Mainland's thick with them." She began to caress Joey's belly.

"Is—is it a nice little cabin, chinked saplings for walls?" he asked hoarsely.

"That's it," Jennifer told him.

"I—we—rode by there today," Joey finished lamely. Sudden he had become worried that he might embarrass himself by exploding under the wonderful treatment they gave him.

"We saw hoofprints, wondered who'd bring horses over here," Judy mused. "Who's the other one?"

"My—ah—stepmother."

"Where's she?" Jennifer asked.

"Out there on that boat. She—ah—has a friend," Joey added.

"Well, what's sauce for the goose is gravy for the gander, eh? Let's get on to the cabin, what say?" Judy urged.

They cut straight through and it took only a short while. Inside, Judy struck a match and lighted a candle. "We like a little light to see by," she explained.

"Th-that's fine with me," Joey replied, eyes filling with the improved view of their lovely bodies.

Jennifer giggled. "You—ah—ever been with a girl before?"

"Uh-huh," Joey admitted.

"Oh, goodie!" Jennifer enthused.

"Ever with two at the same time?" Judy asked coyly.

"Ne-never."

"Then hang on, Joey-honey, we're gonna show you the time of your life," Judy said as she walked over to him.

She circled his neck with her arms and pressed her warm body against his. Her full, sensuous lips covered his and they kissed. Joey quickly became aware of an insistent pressure against his lips and opened to receive

Judy's tongue. They embraced for a long time, interrupted at last by a complaint from Jennifer.

"C'mon, Judy, let me have a turn."

She kissed with equal skill as her twin, Joey soon discovered. The silken touch of her skin on his generated an electric thrill. When they parted, both girls led him to a mattress on the floor.

"Lay down there, Joey-honey," Judy instructed.

Joey did as directed and then they came at him, lips and hands busy with exploring his slender frame. Jennifer squirmed on top of him and he let out a squeal of sheer rapture when she closed her full lips over the heated knob of his member. Judy commenced to lick at the shaft. When he reached the point where he could endure it no longer, the pattern changed.

Judy straddled him and lowered herself until he penetrated her moist cleft and slid deep into the flexing passage. Jennifer sat on his chest, her heady woman aroma making him giddy. The room swirled around Joey and he went blissfully off into oblivion with the two beautiful girls. Time sped by and all thoughts of the real world faded.

Well skilled in the arts of love, Judy and Jennifer taught Joey several new tricks as the long night progressed. He thrust his way to euphoric climaxes time and again with both of them. Such joys were not meant for man to experience he thought to himself by the time their amazing tryst concluded. Drained and weak in the knees, Joey stumbled back to camp with their honeyed promises ringing in his ears to return another night and bring him more pleasure. He reached his makeshift bed only ten minutes ahead of Rebecca and fell into a deep, untroubled slumber.

8

Set in a fold of hills a couple of hundred yards off the main trail between the Texas border and Fort Sill, the Dalkins' road ranch enjoyed a large and steady clientele. The Dalkins brothers employed two bartenders, four bouncers and five soiled doves. Not the most beautiful of women, the painted ladies also doubled as bar-flies to hustle drinks from the passers through. Clock time meant little to the habitués of the Dalkins' establishment.

Day or night found the large, square, low ceilinged main room of the largest building filled nearly to capacity. The three Dalkins brothers lived in a clapboard house next to the saloon, the male employees bunked in a long, narrow structure to the opposite side. Each girl had a room upstairs in which to conduct business and call home. A large barn across the hard packed clearing in front of the road ranch provided livery services for the customers. Business had been going strong for three hours, with noon yet an hour and a half away.

All three Dalkins brothers pitched in to aid the daytime bartender. Music tinkled from an out-of-tune piano and a whiskered old-timer plinked cords on a banjo. Smoke hung in thick, undulating clouds over tables filled with poker players, cowboys swapping tall tales, and hardcases looking for some action. Not a one had danger on his mind when the doors ripped out of their frames and yipping Comanche warriors swarmed through the opening.

"My God, it's Injuns!" Norvil Dalkins shouted.

He bent to retrieve a shotgun from under the bar. An instant later an arrow flashed through the space formerly occupied by his chest. He came up with the sawed-off Greener and put a load of double-aught Buckshot into two warriors. Fifteen .33 caliber balls made gory messes of their chests. Shots from outside indicated the raiding party had more members than those who leaped on customers with tomahawks swinging.

A man's scream cut short when an axe blade cleaved his skull to the bottom of his nose. He spilled forward onto the table and a yelling Comanche bounded over the corpse to find another victim. Gunshots overlapped as the occupants of the saloon unlimbered their weapons and repayed the Indians for their transgressions. Three soiled doves crouched in terror behind the bar.

One trembled as she repeated over and over, "What are we going to do?"

Pierce Dalkins bent low over them. "Shut up and crawl in that cubbyhole in the middle of the back bar and you might live through this."

"I'm scared of small, dark places," one of the whores protested.

"Right now I figure you'd be a lot more scared of Comanches," Pierce snapped.

When she started to answer, her words turned to a scream as Pierce's blood and brains splashed on her face. Pierce dropped his revolver and she snatched it up with alacrity and blew into eternity the Comanche who had killed him with a .45 slug through the breastbone. More hooting savages pushed into the room which had become a slaughterhouse. The bar became a more popular place as patrons vaulted the mahogany top and hunkered down for protection. One young cowboy took in the huddled girls, all three trembling and wide-eyed.

"I'll try an' keep back three bullets, ladies, so's to save you from that fate worse than death."

"Don't bother," one girl told him. "I gave it away for three years before I started to charge when I turned fourteen and ran away from home. I figure I can do it for free again if necessary."

"Dora's right," another soiled dove chimed in. "These Injun bucks ain't got no machinery that different from any other man."

"But they'll torture you, kill you in the end," the youthful drover protested.

An idea formed and the third prostitute produced a tantalizing smile. "Not if we make it real clear we want to party with them. What do you think, girls?"

"I reckon they'd be grateful," Dora responded, "not havin' to wet their wicks in a wildcat."

The white men quickly fell to their attackers. Flames crackled in the Dalkins' house, the bunk room, and barn when the last white man fell with an arrow through his heart. Tired but victorious warriors whooped and improvised little dance steps while they loosened their hair. A stirring behind the bar drew the attention of Stone Knife and some others.

"One of them still lives," a warrior told the leader.

"We will go see," Stone Knife suggested.

Silent in their moccasins, four Comanches approached the bar. A flury of movement stopped them and they stared in consternation. Before them, breasts bared invitingly, stood three fairly comely young women.

"Howdy, boys," Dora said huskily. "How'd you like to take a chew on one of these nice titties? Want to go play pokey-holey? No charge to you brave young fellers."

Stone Knife understood English enough to make out the intent behind the words and lascivious posturing of the females. Knowing what they implied didn't help him to understand it. Troubled by this and plagued by a superstitious fear of some powerful medicine being present, he motioned to his followers to step away from the bar.

"Come," he commanded when he regained control of his voice. "These women are touched by the Spirits. They show their bodies like horses for trading. We will not be stained by their blood."

So saying, he and the others returned to scalping the victims. Then they ran outside and mounted their ponies. Quivering with shock and surprised relief, the trio of harlots clung to each other and wept torrents as the Indian ponies faded off into the distance.

Joey Ridgeway awakened with a big, sappy smile on his face. His groin tingled from the tremendous work out he had undergone the night before. He wanted to sing and shout, jump up and down, skip out into the water for a mile swim. If he could satisfy two utter wantons like Judy and Jenner, he could do *anything*.

He sensed a sudden elongation and rigidity under his loincloth and turned away as Rebecca sat up. She looked at him oddly and shrugged. At his age, she thought, boys have strange reactions to the most ordinary things.

"Good morning. We have some shredded dried beef we can soften and scramble with eggs for breakfast."

"Sounds good," Joey replied absently. Would they come back this night or the next? How could he get away to meet them? Reflecting on it tormented him.

"A morning swim before we eat?" Rebecca queried.

This idea appealed immediately. He could feel the dried stickiness of their combined passion. "Sure. I'll beat you to the water," he challenged.

Rebecca came to her feet, then paused as she saw Carl climb to the foredeck of the *Ulysses* and wave to her. She responded then hurried to the sand, to drop her dress beside Joey's loincloth and sprint into the low wavelets that coursed against the shore. This was turning out to be a marvelous holiday. She felt so pleased that Joey apparently enjoyed it as much as she. She must be doing something right.

Much to their surprise, most of the braves who had given their allegiance to Black Wind, Bear Watcher and Calico Turkey did not agree to go off raiding outside the reservation. Only ten men expressed definite interest. Disgruntled, the Apache war leaders went to talk with Walks Proud. He suggested that a singing be held. All of the Apache men were to be invited, urged to come. There would be plenty to eat, good drummers and words of power and wisdom.

Walks Proud arrived early and supervised the building of a fire. Off to one side, women made acorn cakes — *cah-wey* — and roasted a whole steer over a separate bed of coals. Jugs of *tis-win* went the rounds. Walks Proud did not object to that, but scorned those who asked for the white man's whiskey. At the appointed time, when the men had their bellies full of rich meat, sweet fry bread and acorn cakes, Walks Proud rose and began to harangue them.

"These are the men who follow me. Look on them. See men of courage and dedication. There, our Kiowa brothers. Here the Cheyenne. Here, with Stone Knife, the Comanches. In a short while, I will ask Stone Knife to tell of the latest raid on the whites who sell whiskey inside the Nations. First, I want all to see the scalps taken by Cheyenne, Kiowa and Comanche. Look on them long and think. Then we will help our brothers dance their scalps.

"Those scalps are there for us to welcome because we are strong and brave and will no longer listen to white men's lies. The time has come to act. Join brother with brother and drive the whites out of our land forever."

Deep tones throbbed from the drum and the scalp dance began. Black Wind stood beside Walks Proud and looked on in envy. That could be the *Tloh-ka-dih-nadidah-hae* scalp dance instead of Comanche, he thought with bitter anger. When the dance ended, he and *Ne-pot-on-je* gathered the Apache men close to the front, in a good position to see and hear the speakers.

"Now my brothers and friends, Stone Knife of the Comanches will tell of their latest victory."

Greeted by stamping feet and snapping fingers, Stone Knife took Walks Proud's place and began a long, singsong narrative of the attack on the Dalkins' road ranch. With each phrase, more of the Apache men developed deep interest. Meanwhile, Walks Proud walked off for some distance, into the enveloping blackness of a jumble of rocks and age twisted

92

cottonwoods. There he made a welcoming sign to two men who waited for him.

"I'm surprised to see you here, Nathan," Walks Proud stated in clear, perfect English.

"I wouldn't have come, Simon, except that Mr. Naish was taken suddenly ill and it is an emergency. Let me introduce our associate from New York, Mr. Seymore Roth. His bank is counting heavily upon your success at stirring up the Army into a regular bloodbath," Nathan Benjamin informed Walks Proud.

"Simon Blackthorne, it's a genuine pleasure to make your acquaintance," the New York banker said affably. "Benjamin here, and the Senator, have said so many good things about you. I'm sorry I didn't understand what you told those savages out there, but it surely stirred them up, hee-hee."

Walks Proud speared the short, fat, New York banker with a frigid beam of his ebony eyes. "I want you to keep in mind that those 'savages' are my brothers, Mr. Roth. It ill behooves you to make light of them when you are two hundred and fifty miles or more from safety in any direction."

"My word. I—ah—I'll be more circumspect in the future, be assured of that."

"Oh, I am, Mr. Roth. Now, Nathan, what is this emergency?"

"The Army has been searching for you and somehow got wind of this powwow tonight. They're sending Indian Police to arrest you. They could be here at any time."

"Thank you for the warning, old friend. It would be best if you and this banker left quickly. It's not to our advantage for the Army to learn of your involvement. Oh, I heard from the Senator that you got

93

into some trouble down in Texas," Walks Proud prodded.

"Yes, damnit. Some nosey woman got in the middle of a little enterprise of mine. I was teaching the ropes to the son of an old friend. But, a good lawyer and enough money judiciously spread around can work wonders. Good-bye for now. We'll be in touch."

"Give my regards to the Senator," Walks Proud replied, then turned and walked back to the half circle around the tall rock on which Stone Knife stood to address the reluctant Apaches.

"Here are the newspapers, sir. I acquired them on the mainland when we fetched groceries," Carl Blake's manservant informed him.

"Thank you, Martin. Now we can find out what's been happening in the world."

"For once, I'm in a mood to say, who cares?" Rebecca told him with a light laugh.

Carl and Rebecca sat in the cockpit of the *Ulysses*, enjoying the afternoon sun and sipping lemonade. Carl handed her the *Galveston Record* and he opened a copy of the *Sun*. It took no time at all for Rebecca to find something that provoked her worry.

"Carl, look at this. A lot of people are being killed in Indian Territory. It's not inter-tribal fighting, even the Army has been attacked at a place called Camp Fenton."

"Yes, there's something here about it, too. Damn, this could get out of hand."

"I know what you mean," Rebecca agreed. "Not to sound overdramatic, but the whole frontier could become embroiled in another Indian war. It would—it could mean destruction for all the tribes."

Carl eyed her over the top of his paper. "That is a little dramatic, but yes, I can see where that might come about. There's some hothead leading these attacks. Some Kiowa war chief named Walks Proud. Did you see that?"

"The *Record* says he is really a half-blood named Blackthorne, who tried to stir up trouble in Texas and the Dakotas before this," Rebecca responded.

"There's more to this than what appears and I don't like it one bit," Carl said with such force that Rebecca put down the newspaper and peered thoughtfully at him.

"I was about to say the same thing. We've talked a little about my past," Rebecca began. "You know that despite the bad years, my sympathies still lie with the Indian part of me. Especially after what has happened these last few years. Something like this— this Red Messiah as they're calling him—could cause terrible harm to all the people. Not to mention hundreds, maybe thousands of whites that might die before it ends."

"For my own part," Carl started, almost apologetically, "I'm concerned about those whites. An entire company wiped out at this Camp Fenton. Something has to be done to stop it before worse happens."

Rebecca sighed and looked across the cove to where Joey fished from the canoe. "That's why I intend to go there and look into the situation."

Carl leaned toward her, his body telegraphing his earnestness. "Why don't we take on this project together?"

"Carl, that's impractical. I've had a lot of experience with the Indians. Lived among them, speak Lakota and some Cheyenne. Forgetting the fact I'm a woman, I have faced more than one person's share of danger."

95

"Look, Becky, there has to be more behind thi than just another Indian prophet calling for the ex pulsion of whites from Indian land. It appears from the newspaper accounts that you might need som competent help."

Without thinking, Rebecca blurted, "And an Ox ford Don is going to provide that help?"

For a moment a hurt expression marred Carl' handsome features. "I've been other places beside Oxford, Becky. Remember those two long scars yo asked about way back in Austin? The one along my ribs came from an *assigai* and the one on my abdo men was made by a Zulu cattle knife, both wielded by Zulu warriors."

"Who are the Zulus?" Rebecca asked.

"It was several years ago. Back in 1878, in South ern Natal Province of British South Africa. King Cetshwayo of the Zulus rose up against British rule He and twenty thousand warriors slaughtered five hundred British soldiers at Isandhlwana. Then his re maining fourteen thousand *impe* infested Rorke's Drift for eighteen hours. After that the seven thou sand left went on a real rampage. I was working on an engineering project for the British Army and got wrapped up in the Zulu War. It lasted nearly a year with the Zulus being nearly wiped out as far as fight ing men went. I've been in other dangerous places, in South America, China, even in this country. So I fee capable of doing what's needed in this instance."

"I never suspected," Rebecca offered in apology. "I'm sorry about that snotty remark. Carl, this will be doubly dangerous. The renegade Indians will be our enemy and we'll technically be illegally in Indian Territory so the Army will be after us, too."

Carl produced a satisfied smile. "I notice you're using the plural. Am I to take that as a yes?"

Rebecca made a pensive face. "Provided you answer one question honestly. What exactly do you do that puts you in these dangerous situations?"

Carl soothed his eager expression into a bland front. "A little of this and a little of that. I told you I had worked for the British government, I also did some consulting work for the Argentinians, in Brazil and Venezuela. They're still in the throes of trying to organize operative democracies after expelling the Spanish and Portuguese. It's somewhat rocky down there. And the Monroe Doctrine is in constant jeopardy."

"Who, then, put you in these places?"

Carl put a finger to her lips. "You said one question. Let it be for now, Becky. For the time being, call it personal curiosity and a desire to spend more time with you. I'll have Martin and Trent take the *Ulysses* back to Galveston and we can leave whenever you're ready."

"Joey will be heartsick," Rebecca observed. "So, I suppose, will I. It's been pleasant here. You coming along made it even better. Yet, I know I won't rest easy until I find out more about this uprising in the Nations."

9

What could be called the legitimate part of Bannister existed on the northern, Kansas, side of the border with Indian Territory. The seamy side consisted of a rambling, clapboard, two-story building that housed a saloon, bordello and trading post, with living accommodations for the occupants above the three businesses. The Pawnee Indian Police and Cherokee Light Horse visited it frequently and shut down the illegal operation. It opened immediately upon their departure.

Currently Damon Vice conducted business in the saloon. He was a lecherous fellow, a widower, who was satisfying his lust with fourteen-year-old local girls. On this bright, early morning, Vice occupied himself with working up sufficient concupiscence for another coupling with the latest teenage girl.

Tears ran down her face as she huddled in the wretched jumble of grayed, infrequently washed sheets on her pallet on the floor. Her thin shift had been hiked up to mid-thigh and she clamped her coltish legs together against a spindly arm that she thrust between them to shield her often ravaged passage.

"Please, not again," she begged; her lips atremble. "I don't want to anymore."

A hot light glowed in the eyes of Damon Vice. "Ah, but you did at one time, didn't you? You did the first time we ever, an' you did the last time. You cooed and squealed and told me how good it was."

"I—I couldn't help myself. I-It—it gets all so confused. It's wrong, what we do, but it makes me all weak and giddy. Still, it's wrong and I don't want to do it anymore," she wailed.

"Well, you're gonna have to. There ain't anyone else I want but you," Vice growled, trousers loosened and halfway down his thighs, his swollen organ bulging his underdrawers.

"No! Please, no," she begged, eyes big, frightened, wild.

Ears deaf to a sudden outbreak of shouting outside, Damon Vice advanced on the girl. Boards creaked as footsteps pounded on the stairs. A startled voice shouted a question that ended in a scream. Then the door banged open and three Cheyenne warriors spilled into the room.

"What the hell!" Damon Vice exclaimed a moment before he died horribly, his trousers around his knees and his rigid member in one hand.

Two arrows transfixed him and a .44 caliber ball from an old Colt Dragoon revolver burst his skull. The girl looked at him silently for several seconds.

One of the warriors started toward the bed, her ripe body a beacon he could not ignore. Before he reached her, Pony Nose appeared in the doorway. He made a curt gesture that halted the braves.

"No. Leave her alone," he commanded. "She has suffered enough."

Rapid gunfire broke out across the line in Kansas as the residents and businessmen put up a valiant defense of their property and lives. Pony Nose directed his men outside and turned to the girl.

"He bad man. Get what he deserve." Then he was gone with the others.

Try as she might, the girl found only tears of rejoicing, and not the slightest sense of grief. Faintly she heard the sounds of battle. War whoops echoed in the hall and voices speaking English cursed the Indians.

Outside, dust and powder smoke obscured a scene of bloody slaughter. Bullets cracked through the air and arrows moaned their songs of death. Above the tumult, one man crouched on a roof, behind the false front. He watched the Cheyennes' movements and called out targets.

"Over to the right! They're headin' for the gen'ral store." He took aim at a mounted warrior and squeezed off a round.

His Winchester bucked in his grip and he saw the Cheyenne go down before smoke filled his field of view. He shifted slightly and saw three braves start a dash for the Casper house.

"Jacob, they're coming your way," he shouted.

One by one he watched his friends and family die. Choked with rage and grief, he barely kept a hold on his perch. He could only moan in despair as the last few whites, those who hadn't run away, met their end. When it grew silent, he could not see beyond immediate revenge. Carefully he looked around until he identified the leader. He aban-

100

doned caution to stand and take careful aim at Pony Nose.

His shot went wild when an arrow pierced his gut. Screaming he slid to the edge of the roof and fell two stories to the alley. The sudden stop broke his neck. Pony Nose trotted forward and halted over the sprawled body.

"This was a brave man. We will do him much honor when we dance our scalps. Light no fires in the white lodges. We will ride for the Washita."

All sign of the measles had departed when Rebecca, Joey and Carl reached the Parsons' homestead. Rebecca explained that something important had come up and Amanda readily accepted another mouth to feed under her roof. Joey had been most disappointed about leaving—Judy and Jennifer had come back twice since the first night and he enjoyed each inventive session enormously. Now they became a part of his past.

"I figure you'd enjoy visiting here the last few days of your holiday, rather than return to Merrill's early," Rebecca told Joey on the day she and Carl were to leave.

Joey's eyes twinkled. "Oh, yeah. I'll like it a whole lot." He caught a glance of anticipation from Winonna. "It would have been fun, though, if we could have stayed on the island."

Mildly puzzled, Rebecca remarked rhetorically, "I had no idea that you would find so much pleasure in being there."

"I did, oh, I sure did," Joey enthused. "I—can we go back some time?"

"Next summer? Would you like that?" Rebecca asked.

101

"And how! Well," he resumed his sober demeanor. "I suppose this is good-bye."

"I'll miss you, Joey. We had such a good time together."

After all the good-byes had been said and she and Carl rode off to take the train as far north as possible, to Dallas, Rebecca's mood changed somewhat. She thought ahead to what they might find and reflected on past situations where Indian and white had clashed. It kept her somber until they secured their horses in a stock car and boarded the Texas & Pacific local to Dallas.

"No Pullman car," Rebecca observed.

"And no handy little room, I'll bet you," Carl mourned.

Rebecca grew an impish expression. "I'll wager we'll find a way."

They did, briefly and ecstatically, standing up on the vestibule between the second class and baggage cars. Not the most satisfying trysting place but the risk made it exciting. In Dallas they added two packmules to their entourage and set off northward for Indian Territory.

Intchi-Dijin stood before the gathered, restless Apache young men. His scowl reflected his impatience with them. *Ne-pot-on-je* and *Wano-boono* flanked the edges of the gathering. Black Wind spoke in low, intense tones, telling again of the promises of Walks Proud. Time passed and the fire grew low. Gradually he saw a change come over some in the group. The siren call of the Red Messiah began to work its spell over them. Black Wind allowed himself to grow hopeful.

"How many of you like to live here as the whites

102

want us to?" No hands raised. "Who would rather fight like a man and die like a warrior than to grow soft and fat and old, half starved and sick with the white man's diseases?" Again not a hand. "You have all pledged yourselves to us," his sweeping arm included Bear Watcher and Calico Turkey. "Now we call on you to honor those pledges."

Persuasion was suddenly taken from *Intchi-Dijin* and his fellow leaders, and decision was wrested from their listeners. Indian Police and a squad of soldiers rushed in out of the dark and arrested them all. A brisk march over seven miles brought the disgruntled Apaches to the main post stockade at Fort Sill.

"Search 'em all good again," Sgt. Mayhew commanded. "Then put these vermin in the stockade."

Two days passed and they had gone well into the third night in the prison compound when one of the staunchest doubters overcame his shame enough to approach Black Wind. *"Intchi-Dijin,* you are right. The bluecoats only wish to keep us in this unhealthy place until we all sicken and die. The White Father in *Was-i-tona* no longer wants to see *Tindé* walk the land. *Tengo mucho vergüenza,"* he summed up in Spanish. "I have much shame," he repeated, his emotions too powerful for his own tongue. "We will go with you, follow the way of Walks Proud, be free men again."

Quickly a plan grew out of observations Black Wind and his chief lieutenants had made during their captivity. Six of the Apaches set to work fashioning ropes from torn strips of blanket. For added resilience they braided in long strands of their hair. Expectation grew as the large coils increased in

103

length. Midnight found the guards drowsy and in-attentive. One jailer, unarmed, patrolled the cell-blocks, four more walked the platform around the inner walls of the stockade. The rest slept until their tour every two hours.

Apache eyes watched them make their rounds. More warriors bided the time until they would act. Black Wind supervised it all. He longed for a *sotol* lance, a good bow and a strong horse between his legs. To be in such a place was to be less than a man. The humiliation the white soldiers had heaped upon him burned like flaming oil. Gradually his thoughts turned to his woman, his children. Had the Indian Police taken them captive also?

No, he had heard that the soldier-chief, Britton, had a soft heart for children and would not do such a thing. "Is it true?" he put his thoughts into words.

"What is that?" Calico Turkey asked.

"It it true that our families will be safe, not harmed, even if we get away and join Walks Proud?"

"The soldier-chief has said it," Calico Turkey assured him. "It is known by those who have long been in this place that the soldier-chief does not lie."

"Unnh. Then what we do is good. Come, all is about ready."

A young brave, chosen for his good looks and still boylike physique, lay on a straw mat. Black Wind smeared a daub of human feces on his legs and two Apaches urinated around the prone figure. It would give him the smell of one near death. Splashes of water on his face and chest simulated a fever in full sweat. At Black Wind's signal he began to writhe and groan.

After a couple of minutes, Black Wind set up a call in Spanish and English for help. "He is very sick," he complained. "Hurry, bring a medicine healer."

Grumbling, the jailer worked his way through the parallel cell locks to the rear corner where the Apache prisoners were confined at night. He saw the groaning young man on the filthy mattress and at once opened the door. With crude sign language he got his message across.

"You two, bring him out."

Bear Watcher and another warrior did as instructed. They came out with the boy, followed in a rush by the rest of the Apaches. The stunned guard went down without a cry. Quickly the freed Indians reached the doorway and Black Wind used the example of a key in the lock to open their cell to gain their way to freedom through a door in the back wall of the prison.

"Go now," Black Wind instructed the four men responsible for elimanating the walking sentries.

They moved with liquid silence. Dark shadows appeared on the palisade around the military detention center. Swiftly they merged with the silhouettes of the guards and in brief, magic lantern plays of quiet violence, the soldiers went down. Black Wind made a choppy gesture with one arm.

"Now. Up there with the ropes. Hurry," he commanded the men involved.

In little time the four lengths of braided blanket material dangled down the outside of the stockade. The thirty warriors and their leaders blended with the night as they slid down and made their way between the buildings of the main post and out into the country.

"First we will steal horses," Black Wind told them once away from any chance of detection. "Then we get guns and join Walks Proud."

No word of protest answered him this time.

Livid in his anger, Lt. Gen. Albert Britton addressed his staff and regimental commanders in an icily controlled voice. "Am I to understand that thirty-three Apaches, whom we managed to arrest with only a handful of Indian Police, have escaped from the stockade?"

"Yes, sir," Col. Trask answered dolefully. "Less than half an hour ago."

"We took casualties." It was a statement not a question.

"Yes, General. Three men dead, two seriously injured," Trask reluctantly informed him.

"I will not accept this," Gen. Britton thundered. "I want all of the Apaches on the reservation rounded up and contained in the stockade. I want Gatling guns mounted and the watch quadrupled. Double the patrols searching for Walks Proud and his hostiles. Set our Delaware and Osage scouts on the trail of the escaped hostiles. Follow them with an entire regiment, with a battery of artillery. They should lead us to Walks Proud and then we can bring this to an end."

"Sir, a question," Col. Lydell Simms asked primly.

"Go ahead, Lydell," Gen. Britton acknowledged, certain he knew what would be said.

"Why this sudden change in position, sir? Only a

106

few days ago you spoke eloquently about maintaining a climate of peace—should we say, business as usual—among the non-hostile agency Indians. You rejected the idea of mass arrests. Now . . ." He left it open with a smirk.

Gen. Brittons eyes narrowed. "All positions are flexible. Lydell, you of all people should know this. As to details, I'll discuss it with you privately after this meeting. George," he said to an aide, "arrange coffee for us, if you please."

"Yes, sir," the young lieutenant responded. "With a bit of brandy, sir?"

"Definitely," Britton snapped. "Now, gentlemen, let's get to details. Hopkins, you may dismiss your adjutant now and have him notify and activate the companies of your regiment. They will be following the trackers. Jones, your Third Battery will accompany them, see they are alerted immediately. The rest of you will draw plans for doubling the number of patrols from your regiments. Do it right here, now. Also I want you to arrange from out of your headquarters companies of men to double the guard complement at the stockade." Gen. Britton paused a moment; thinking, he paced to a blackboard and back to the long, oak table.

"Before we begin the roundup of the Apaches, send Capt. Herndon to Chief Jay. Herndon speaks the language. Have him, for want of a better word, provide some diplomatic reason for the roundup. It only need be effective enough to prevent any of the Apaches slipping off before we surround them and bring them here to Main Post."

Col. Lydell Simms made it clear by his expression how he felt about not having his regiment selected to pursue the renegade Apaches. He sat in

107

brooding silence, with clear indication that he paid
not the least attention to the rest of Gen. Britton's
plans. Those seated beside him marked the tight
bulge of muscle at the hinges of his jaw as he
clenched his teeth.

10

No one lived here. That much became obvious over the passage of time and miles. It made the desolate scrubland of this ill defined no-man's-land between north Texas and Indian Territory even more forbidding. Rebecca Caldwell reined in and gazed across the sun-browned expanse. Soon snow would cover this sere plain, she mused. A thick blanket would wipe out any possibility to identify landmarks and determine one's location.

"Are we still in Texas?" she asked.

That brought a sharp bark of laughter from Carlton Blake. "I was about to ask you the same question. I'm not certain, and we'll pay hell asking anyone from the looks of it."

"Then we keep going north," Rebecca determined.

"For how long?" Carl queried.

"Until we encounter someone," she speculated.

"It might be one of the hostiles," Carl offered.

"In which case we can begin our work of bringing an end to all this." Rebecca indicated her clothing with a graceful sweep of one hand and arm. "I usually travel this way in unsettled country. It has its advantages in more than comfort. I think I can guarantee that we'd at least be given a hearing, rather than killed outright."

Carl gave careful examination of her red-brown, doeskin dress, Sioux moccasins, braided hair and beadwork. "That's reassuring," he said with little conviction.

"Oh, Carl, relax a little. For all your worldly adventures, I gather the distinct impression that you participated within the structure of a military force or government department of some sort. This is obviously a different undertaking. Trust me. I've gone about it this way from the start."

"With what results beside staying alive?" He sought reassurance, not to belittle her.

"All forty-some of the Bitter Creek Jake Tulley gang are in jail, graves, or otherwise relegated entirely to history. They simply aren't any more. And there are others. Roger Styles, a number of unconnected outlaws, corrupt politicians and military men. For one thing it gets people to lower their guard when they appear to be dealing with a half-Indian woman. After all, what can she do?"

Carl chuckled and took time for a brief swallow from his canteen. "Good thing there's lots of streams in this area. This country could be nasty in the middle of summer. A lot like north-eastern Natal, or the Argentine Pampas."

"I hope this romantic streak remains until we make camp tonight," Rebecca teased as she gigged *Sila* into a gentle trot. An hour more on the trail brought them to a gently rising escarpment that revealed at its edge the steep slope that led to the flood plain of the Red River. To Rebecca's surprise a well-worn, though narrow, trail led down the concave face of the syncline plate. In the distance, beyond the river, she made out the dark, irregular, boxlike silhouettes that implied buildings.

"There's some sort of settlement up ahead," she informed Carl. "This must be the Red, so that means the buildings are in the Nations."

"Given an easy crossing of the river, we should be there within an hour," Carl opined after studying the terrain.

Jonah Deerhorn made a good living operating the only ferry to cross the Red between Texas and Indian Territory. He happened to be on the north side of the river, whittling, enjoying a chew, and drinking a few beers, when the bell rang to announce passengers waiting on the Texas side. Grumbling, he laid aside his stick and knife and looked across the cinnamon-colored water.

His old eyes made out a man and woman waiting. Not a hell of a big fee, but the woman looked Indian. Might do to find out what went on. "Jeeter," he called to his yellow dog, that lay half in the water to keep cool. "We're goin' back."

With a shower of droplets, the dog jumped aboard and shook itself. Jonah lifted the pall and snapped a buggy whip over the rump of the scrawny mule hitched to the crossbar of a capstan. The animal protested noisily and began to walk the restricted circle on the forepeak of the barge. Since most of his business went from Texas to the Nations, Jonah chose to drift with the current to the north bank and winch back across empty. Loud squeaking came from the drum as the rope tautened and began to slide through a hawsehole and wrap on the spindle on the deck below.

Halfway across, Jonah made quick appraisal of the quality of their clothes and revised his fee schedule. "That'll be two bits apiece," he told his customers as they started to board the ferry vessel.

111

"Sort of stiff, isn't it?" the apparent squaw woman asked in perfect English. Her astonishing blue eyes disturbed Jonah.

"When you got the only game in town, Missy, you can charge whatever you want for openers," Jonah cackled philosophically. "Come or go as you please."

"We'll ride with you," Rebecca told him. "Those buildings over there, what settlement is it?"

"It ain't. That's Fat Jack's. It's a road ranch, whatever you want to call it. Jack's got him a saloon and a trading post, livery barn where he does a bit of blacksmithin', shoes horses when the mood strikes him."

"Thank you," Rebecca responded coolly to the news. To Carl, "We do need some supplies. And I could use a stove cooked meal."

"We'll do it, then," Carl agreed.

"I wouldn't iffin I was you," Jonah advised. He gave them a sly look and a wink. "There's some fellers there think they're a law unto themselves."

"How do you mean that?" Carl asked.

Jonah cackled and rolled his eyes. "Oh, you'll find out, sure as there's the Devil, you'll know what I mean." They could get nothing more out of him.

Crossing the Red provided an ample day's supply of excitement. The barge swayed downstream between two thick guide ropes, the rapid current threatening to tip the flat boat at any moment. With the gear disengaged, the tow rope fed out with a disconcerting screech over the polished facing of the hawsehole. Rebecca spent considerable energy calming her Palouse stallion. The packmules stolidly accepted the novel means of transportation.

On the opposite shore, Rebecca and Carl coaxed the animals off the frail looking vessel and mounted. Unsure of the boatman's meaning, they approached

112

the tumbledown collection of buildings with heightened senses. They reached their goal uneventfully.

A couple of hard-faced individuals lounged outside the saloon. They gave the newcomers a going over from eyes cold and blank. Rebecca shrugged it off as they knocked dust from their clothes and stepped up on the sagging porch.

Rebecca and Carl approached the sagging doorway where a sign announced Fat Jack's Trading Post. Tall, narrow double doors, with grimy panels of glass, stood open and inviting—if such a word could be applied to Fat Jack's. They entered and found the proprietor behind a counter that consisted of rough sawed planks atop barrels. Several glass cases rested on this and barrels with hatch-lid tops sat at random around the room. They saw at once that the "fat" in the owner's name was neither a fiction nor a brag.

He must have weighed three hundred pounds. His arms bulged like hams, his belly a wide expanse like an inland sea. A big moon face beamed welcome at them.

"Howdy, folks. You comin' or goin'?"

"Coming, I suppose you could say," Carl informed him.

"We need to replenish our supplies," Rebecca added.

"Seems you've got some supplies out there now that's plum illegal," a voice announced from behind them. "Contraband as they say."

They turned to face the newcomer. "Whatever gave you that idea," Carl demanded.

"More to the point," Rebecca demanded, "what gave you the idea you could poke around in our possessions?"

"Why, Missy, I'm the law around these parts," the tall, rail-thin, gaunt faced individual announced.

113

"Fact is, most everything you brought in here is contraband."

"That's a crock," Carl growled.

The dark, sinister faced man raised his left hand in a cautioning gesture. "Now don't go gettin' riled, Mister. That is, if you like breathin'."

"He's right, folks," Fat Jack wheezed. "You oughtta pay some attention to what he says."

"That sounded like a threat," Rebecca stated. "And I would like to point out there's only one of you."

"Wrong!" he contradicted with a ringing tone. "There's five of us. Four of my boys have confiscated your horses and the — ah — contraband and are waiting right outside."

"Since you're the law around here, what comes next?" Carl asked in a lazy drawl that dripped insolence.

"You admit to smuggling, whereupon all your gear is confiscated, you pay the fine, then if you want horses, saddles, any other tack and supplies, buy them from Fat Jack here," the gaunt hardcase advised through a snicker.

"Buy back our own property?" Rebecca asked, incredulously. At the shakedown artist's nod her expression grew hard and grim. "Not goddamn likely!"

Such an expression, coming so harshly, from so attractive a young woman had the desired shock effect. The two-bit extortionist hadn't even reached the grips of his Colt .45 before he looked down the muzzle of a Colt Bisley in Rebecca's hand. Carl covered Fat Jack, who had abruptly stopped snickering.

"Why don't we go have a talk with your fellow scum?" Rebecca prompted.

She stepped forward and slid the Colt .45 from his holster, then prodded him with her weapon. They crossed to the door and out into the sunlight. Four men stood around their horses and packmules. When they saw their leader apparently a prisoner, one went for his gun.

Rebecca coolly shot him in the belly and he went to the ground on his knees. His round split shingles from the underside of the porch overhang a moment before he dropped his revolver. Confused and startled by the shots, the other three also drew. Rebecca stepped behind the hardcase she had disarmed and he shouted in fright.

"No, don't!"

Two bullets smashed into his chest, which caused a spray of blood and bits of cloth to form in the air. He took a tottering step forward, groaned and pitched face first onto the ground, in a puddle of horse urine. Carl fired through the doorway and downed another of the gunmen. He turned back in time to put a hot slug in Fat Jack's shoulder. The huge man cried in anguish and dropped the shotgun he'd retrieved from under the counter.

Weighing the situation, the remaining pair of toughs dropped their weapons and raised their hands. "We give up," one babbled in a rush.

"Yeah, we don't want none of this. You got us cold," his more loquacious friend declared.

"Step up here to these porch posts," Rebecca commanded. They obeyed with alacrity. "Now, put your backs to them and face the road. Put your arms behind them."

"You boys stay there while she does what she wants," Carl added as he came out with a blubbering Fat Jack.

Rebecca took some short coils of rope from a saddlebag and returned to the porch. Quickly, with accomplished skill, she tied the men's wrists so they

115

would have to lift the whole porch roof to get free. Then she glanced over at Fat Jack.

"We'll take those supplies now," she said without a ruffle.

"B-but I'm—I'm hurt; shot. You gotta patch me up," the obese merchant whined.

Rebecca's cobalt eyes turned icy. "The only thing we've gotta do is let you live. Keep talking and that won't even figure."

"Jesus. You're a hard biddy," Fat Jack gulped. "Damn' squaw wimmin."

"You hold that thought while you fill our order," Rebecca commanded.

Fat Jack did so, swiftly if not willingly. Carl paid for their purchases and sat the crooked trader on the floor embracing one of the counter barrels. Then he tied Fat Jack's hands and feet.

"B-b-but I'll bleed to death," Fat Jack wailed.

Rebecca examined the slow seep of blood from his wound. "You won't," she stated flatly. "The ferry-man heard the shots. He'll be here before long to find out what happened."

"Jesus—oh Jesus. Nobody's gonna believe this. Spike Filcher dead, along with two of his boys, and another pair tied up to my porch. Jesus!"

Outside, Rebecca shook off the last of her keyed-up reflexes. "You went through that without a word of a plan, Carl. Had all the right moves. I'm impressed."

Carl's lips twisted into a rueful pucker. "Think I'm qualified to ride along now?"

Rebecca shook her head. "And then some. Let's go before some of their friends show up."

Beaver Canyon on the Washita River in Indian Teritory: great slashes of yellow, umber and chocolate that the flowing river had carved out eons before the first man walked along the bank. Throbbing drum-beats echoed off the walls, swelled and ebbed to a man-made tempo. Strangely, though, it seemed a part with nature, not an alien presence. A large ring of rocks, deeply filled with glowing coals, formed the focal point. Over it slowly rotated a whole steer and four pigs on green wooden spits. Savory odors rose from the meat.

There would be a big feasting later. First Walks Proud would speak to the many warriors he had summoned there. The beat of the drums changed, became more energetic. Men who had been on recent raids began to dance, each acted out his feats of valor. Others looked on enviously. When the drummers and singers signaled their desire for a break, Walks Proud climbed to the flat top of a boulder that put him half of his height above the thick throng of young men. He raised his hands for silence. When the furthest out quieted down, he took a deep breath and projected his voice so all could hear.

"I asked you here so you could feast with us, fill your bellies like the lying white man's rations could never do. I also asked you here to see the truth, to marvel over it and to join me. I have come to a way of proving my invincibility.

"All who will join me in sweat lodges, purify yourselves! Drink no more of the white man's whiskey. Let me give you my secret words and we will fight in a great victory over the white enemy. Their bullets will not touch you, their long knives will not cut you. I will ride at the forefront of our attack and not a hair of my head will be harmed."

Through whoops and yelps, several voices demanded, "When will we fight? Where will the white's die?"

"We are going to attack Camp Cobb."

A sudden, collective gasp came from the assembly. Camp Cobb had many white soldiers there. A strong place with spiked walls and long-shooting guns. Voices of objection began to rise.

"No. They are too strong."

"We are not enough warriors."

"The bluecoats will kill us all."

Even some of Walks Proud's most fanatic followers scowled and muttered among themselves. Big Belly, Pony Nose, Stone Knife and Black Wind pushed through the gathered fighting men and stood before the leader. Frowns gullied their foreheads.

"You ask too much," Stone Knife challenged.

"We must make the pony soldiers come out to fight, then we will beat them," Pony Nose suggested.

"Listen—listen to me. All of you, hear my words. My medicine is strong, it grows more powerful each day. We cannot lose. We will make our plans and ride out from this canyon two days from now. Then the white invaders will pay dearly and we shall not even bleed."

11

From a distance it appeared to be a small, black cloud that boiled with fierce internal pressures, while it remained stationary. By mid-afternoon of their first day in Indian Territory, the strange object could be seen clearly on the horizon. Two hours' ride brought them close enough that Rebecca Caldwell could make out the individual elements of the whirling mass. She turned her face to Carl Blake with an unpleasant expression.

"Something's dead up there. Rather *a lot* of something, I'd say. I've never seen so many buzzards in flight before."

"A grim sight, I'll agree," Carl allowed. "There are no towns in this part of the Nations, so what do you expect to find?"

"We've come nearly a day's journey from the border. This seems a likely spot for some sort of inn or tavern, a place to rest for the night."

Carl gave her a neutral grin. "Aren't you ascribing some highly organized, civilized customs to the Indians who inhabit this country?"

"The 'civilized' ones would definitely want overnight lodgings, the 'wild' ones, if the term still applies, wouldn't care," Rebecca replied, conscious she

119

must sound like someone giving a lecture. "White men, on the other hand, even troops, would welcome a small taste of civilization. Particularly a good stiff drink in an area where liquor is prohibited by law."

"Your point is well taken. We're bound to find out in a short while anyway."

When they reached the blackened ruins, the general layout of what had been four or five buildings appeared consistent with the plans of stagecoach relay stations they had visited in the past as well as Fat Jack's road ranch.

"Poor devils," Carl opined as he examined the ravaged human remains, "it looks like they didn't have a chance."

"Indians, definitely," Rebecca stated as she examined the scene. "I'm no expert of fires and their causes," she went on, "but it appears to me that the Comanches who did this didn't drink up the whiskey before they burnt the place down. See how hot the blaze must have been in the saloon? Nothing but white ash. Something fueled that fire longer than the rest and I'm willing to bet it was alcohol."

"What sort of raiding hostiles refrain from getting drunk when they have the chance?"

"I don't know, Carl. We'll have to find out about that, and a lot of other things, before we can be useful in stopping this marauding. There's nothing we can do here. Might as well put some distance between this and us before we camp for the night."

They rode on until the sun rested like a big orange ball on the flat line of the western horizon. Following Oglala custom, Rebecca suggested they make camp in a dry wash, well below the flat plain of southern Indian Territory, out of sight of any watchers or passersby.

Once situated, she built a small fire of twigs and

uffalo chips, one assured of being smokeless. Only
few thin, white wisps rose above the first tentative
ames, and then disappeared entirely. Overhanging
anks kept its glow from being readily seen at any
istance. Carl tended the horses and lugged over the
ooking gear and food box.

"Now that we're here, I feel somewhat like we're on
fool's errand," he declared.

"How's that?" Rebecca asked.

"The sensible thing is to go to the Army. But we
ave no authorization to do that. Where do we find
he hostiles? More to the point, what do we do once
ve have?"

"First off, I thought we could go among the peace-
ble tribes, talk to the elders. That way we can learn
ll we can about the strength of the hostile force;
vho is a part of it; where they might be found. Then
ve can decide how to handle it. As a last chance, I'd
ay we go to the Army and tell them where to find
he hostiles." Rebecca paused and frowned. "That
vill lead to a lot of killing on both sides. I'd prefer to
ind a peaceful solution."

"With Walks Proud involved, I tend to doubt the
hance of that," Carl told her. He sighed and started
on another tack. "You never cease to surprise me,
Becky. When we were in settled parts of the country,
you were the model of a sophisticated woman. You
wore stylish clothes with a real flair, spoke and acted
ike one would expect. Out here, in that beaded dress
and moccasins, your hair in braids, you are the con-
summate Indian woman. Your trail skills and track-
ng sense are remarkable. You make camp quickly
and simply, and you project a strong Indian affinity
with the way Indians think. It's almost as though you
were two people."

Rebecca ducked her head to hide a slight blush. "I

121

take your remarks as compliments, Carl. I hope I'm not wrong in that."

"You're not. Now then," he began in yet another direction as he squatted beside her at the fire, "what did you have in mind for after we eat?"

Rebecca put an arm over Carl's right shoulder and closed fingers on the back of his neck. Slowly she drew him to her. Her cobalt eyes held a deep glow, reflecting the flames in orange-gold sparks.

"I thought . . . we might . . . find the stars . . . rather—ah—enthralling. We could—well, you know."

"Ummm. I think I do." Carl turned slightly and put both of his arms around her. "I also think there's no reason we need to wait until after supper to find out."

Carl hugged her to his chest with a fierceness born of passion and possessiveness. *His* woman. *His* beautiful white squaw. He had known many women in his life from that first splendorous awakening of his youthful drive at an age when most boys still occupied themselves with marbles, slingshots and rabbit hunting. Still in knee pants, he had literally stumbled into a well-appointed brothel on New York's Lower East Side.

Carl smiled over Rebecca's shoulder as he recalled that unbelievable time. The girls had made much of his smooth, boyish face. Scantily dressed, they soon aroused a sensation heretofore unknown to little Carl Blake. In the end, they squabbled over him, and cut cards. One voluptuous redhead only a few years older than him won out. In her room Carl had his first passionate kiss, lost first his clothes then his innocence. He never knew anything could feel so good.

In the sixteen years since, Carl never stinted in entering contests of the heart. Still two years short of thirty, Carl had recently begun to suspect he had be-

ome jaded. Then he encountered Rebecca Caldwell.
Whole new vistas of erotic pleasure opened for him.

"You're so very precious," he whispered as he un-
tied the laced bindings at the back of her doeskin
dress.

"And you're enough man to make any three
women happy," Rebecca told him sincerely.

"Why, then, we need to get two more women, eh?"
Carl teased.

"I'll scratch their eyes out," Rebecca riposted, joining in the farce.

"Do I detect a tinge of jealousy?"

"You do," Rebecca answered as she fumbled with
the buttons of Carl's shirt.

Soon they had shed clothes and lay on a blanket
near the fire ring. Flickering orange light illuminated
Carl's lean, hard body as he lowered himself between
Rebecca's supple limbs. Widespread legs gave easy
access to the pouting cleft that bisected her puffy
mound. The big, broad tip of his rigid organ brushed
lightly over the sparse, raven covering. Rebecca shivered and reached for his hips.

"Oh, hurry, Carl. Take me."

Carl's firm, thick fingers parted the outer veils and
he thrust forward, finding instant resistance in the
low relaxation of the slippery walls. Rebecca
groaned and forced herself to slacken enough to accommodate his mighty shaft. Atremble, she received
him in increments, shuddering with each advance.
Little, quivering sounds escaped with each with-
drawal. It took a long while at this pace to reach the
optimum penetration.

"You are truly unlike any other woman," Carl
complimented, enjoying the tightly clinging walls
that encased his member.

"I could say the same about you as a man,"

123

Rebecca admitted softly. "Only words fail to describe . . . the overwhelming presence of—of . . ."

Carl made a long, swift thrust and words fled from Rebecca. She moaned and ground her pelvis and shoved in reply. Slowly their tempo built. The sky above filled with stars, twinkling points of faraway light that shifted and spun as the joy of their coupling robbed Rebecca of clear focus. She thrashed her head from side to side and her eyes went glassy.

"Oh! Oooh, more, Carl, more," she wailed.

Rebecca raised her legs so that she could have greater purchase, shoving herself to him by the power of her feet and legs. Carl swooped and swayed, thrilling and giving joy beyond any previous experience even with Rebecca.

"Becky—Becky—Becky—Becky," he chanted as he drove them further from reality.

When the pinnacle had been gained and the wild downward spiral carried them into oblivion, the sky returned to normal and they clasped each other tightly for several long minutes.

"I need to freshen up, get dressed and fix supper," Rebecca excused herself.

"How are you going to do that?"

Rebecca gave him a stern stare. "I've cooked a meal before, Carl."

His hearty laughter cheered them both. "What about after supper? What then?" he coaxed.

"Why—well, I—I suppose . . . more of the same, if you're up to it," Rebecca responded coyly.

"Am I? You wait and see," Carl crowed gleefully, a promise of future bliss.

"We've been sending out doubled patrols for a week and no results," Col. Lydell Simms complained to Lt. Gen. Albert Britton.

124

"Oh, I wouldn't say that. We've established where Walks Proud definitely is *not*. Also which tribes have remained on their agencies, which young men from several agencies have gone hostile, and at least a partial pattern to the raids being made by Walks Proud's followers. I consider that a lot."

"Begging the General's pardon, Albert, but I consider it a colossal waste of time." Simms, hands behind his back, paced before Britton's desk in the headquarters building at Ft. Sill.

"Meaning what, Lydell?" Gen. Britton asked coldly.

"That given the freedom to do it my way, there isn't a day that I couldn't take a hundred men and ride out there and take Walks Proud by the nose."

Briefly Lt. Gen. Britton looked amused, then a frown of impatience creased his brow. "Lydell, do you recall a certain captain named Fetterman? He felt the same way about the Sioux."

"Those were wild Indians," Simms dismissed. "We have a captive audience, if you will."

"A boy of twelve, young Crazy Horse as a matter of fact, suckered Fetterman. He fell for the boy's ruse and wound up dying with his entire command."

"The tactics were Red Cloud's," Simms snapped.

"Not entirely so. For their part, the main body of Sioux, and a few Cheyenne who were along for a hunt, didn't have the slightest idea that Fetterman would lead his troops out onto a spear of elevated land that gave them no clear field of fire against the enemy. But this is not the time to discuss ancient tactics. What I'm trying to point out is that we have no Red Cloud, nor a Crazy Horse. Not even a Sitting Bull. But we do have Walks Proud. He is a clever tactician and somewhat of a strategist as well. I'm inclined to respect the man. That doesn't

125

say I don't want him captured and eliminated.

"However, Lydell, it also doesn't mean I'm willing to let you go out there indiscriminately killing Indian women and children until someone among them tells you where to find Walks Proud."

"Why not? It's been proven to work."

Gen. Britton produced an expression of impatience. "That's where my reference to Fetterman comes in, Lydell. Because while you were busy torturing and killing innocents, Walks Proud would sneak up and shove his war lance up your ass." Swiftly drained of his irritability, the general went on, "I will grant you one thing. There's too much delay in reporting patrol results and coordinating it. I want you to take your regiment into the field and establish a secondary search headquarters at Camp Cobb. Alert your regiment and be ready to ride from Sill at once."

Jimmy and Tommy Hays, aged 12 and 10 respectively, had been born on the family farm along the Washita River. Their mother, Mary Tallgrass, an Osage woman, had married their father, Buck Hays, in Kansas a year before he moved to the Nations. Buck was a big, jolly fellow with broad shoulders, sandy brown hair and big blue eyes. He laughed a lot and had taught his sons to swim before they could reliably walk.

Under his tutelage they had also learned to ride with the ease of a Cheyenne, plant and tend a garden that produced bountiful crops of squash, beans, corn, okra and pokeweed. They also discovered the mysteries of swine and horse breeding and assisted at farrowing time and when foals came. On this bright, unseasonably warm fall day, they finished their chores early and set off with fishing poles, worms and a desire to wet more than their feet in the Washita.

Fluent in both English and Osage, the boys often mixed-up words and concepts in their speech. After two hours of unproductive angling, Tommy complained to his elder brother.

"Jimmy, we've been at this for a hand span of the sun. Not a nibble. I wanna swim."

His elder brother grinned impishly. "So do I. Last one in the water's a dog fart."

"Ugh! That *stinks,*" Tommy complained through his giggles.

Quickly the boys yanked in their lines and stripped to the buff. Jimmy beat Tommy by only half a body length into the cooling water of the Washita. Their heads broke surface a moment later to discover a frequent occurrence, yet one that greatly disturbed them this time.

A dozen riders sat their ponies on the west bank. Each wore only the bare essentials and all were heavily armed. They remained silent; black, beady eyes fixed on the youngsters. All wore war paint.

"Is that the white man's lodge?" Big Belly asked in Kiowa.

Not understanding the words, Jimmy replied in Osage, "No. It's our father's place."

Switching to that language, Big Belly asked, "Who is your father?"

"Buck Hays," Tommy answered.

Instantly Jimmy had a premonition that his brother should not have answered in that manner. "Our mother is Mary Tallgrass, of the Osage people," he rushed to answer.

It made little difference to Big Belly. He nodded toward the boys and two warriors with bows loosed arrows that pierced their smooth, skinny chests. Jimmy make feeble twitches for a moment and Tommy made gargling sounds. Their rich blood stained the Washita.

"Come on, we ride to the lodge, kill the rest," Big Belly commanded.

Two small, lifeless forms slid down on the current after their passage; turning lazily, changing head for toe, sun on their coppery skin and the arrow points protruding from young backs. Neither boy heard the rattle of gunfire that ended their father's life, nor their mother's screams of pain and rage as the Kiowa warriors had their way with her before cutting out her heart.

12

Carl Blake caught Rebecca Caldwell by one hand and pulled her down the embankment onto the strand and along toward a bend in the Washita River. Only a short distance beyond their intended campsite for the evening, the protruding bluff hid his surprise from her until they rounded its base. Then Carl pointed to a huge, twisted, old cottonwood tree.

Its massive base must have been eleven feet in diameter and thick, gnarled limbs spread to shade a wide gully where a smaller stream joined the shallow river. A few of the highest leaves had already turned gold or pale yellow. This was not what Carl pointed to next.

"See it? Right there in the branches. Look carefully."

"What is it, Carl? Did some kind of building get washed down into that tree in a flood?"

"No," Carl said impatiently. "It's a house in the tree. Some one built the biggest, most complete, playhouse I've ever seen. I—I always wanted one as a boy," his voice sounded distant, plaintive. "Even tried to build one with some friends. It was a disaster. But this . . . it's a regular mansion. Come on, I'll show you."

129

Eager as a boy, Carl brought Rebecca to the bank and she removed her moccasins. Already barefoot, Carl took the lead in wading the river over a bed of smooth rocks and soft sand. On the far shore he took Rebecca by both hands and stared deeply into her eyes.

"Now, look above you."

She did and caught her breath. "Oh, Carl, it's incredible. So big, so well built. Someone must have put in a lot of time on this."

"And love. You can't build a place like this without a lot of love."

A thick length of knotted rope hung from a window in a clapboard wall. Farther around the base of the tree a ladder of board strips had been nailed to the trunk. Carl assisted Rebecca on to the first rung, then waited a moment and followed when she ascended. Her trim ankles disappeared into the arboreal mansion and Carl hurried after.

"Carl, this is something out of a dream. It's more than anything some children might have built."

"Definitely. There are four rooms on this level, three above, then two on the third level. One each on three more levels, each one a big room. Come on, I'll show you."

Ladders of the same material as the main access led to each of the branched-out stories. From a window in the topmost, they could look out over the level prairie above the river banks. Appearing close because of its size, a bloated magenta sun lowered toward a horizon made purple-black by a line of storm clouds. Carl and Rebecca remained on their knees a bit longer, gauging the time. Carl put an arm around her shoulder.

130

"We've got maybe an hour to sunset," he murmured in her ear.

"Ummmm. Delightful," Rebecca replied.

She slipped out of Carl's embrace and stood. In the red-orange glow she removed her Sioux dress and displayed her breathtaking curves and hollows. Her faintly copper skin seemed to radiate a light of its own. Carl responded to her invitation with alacrity.

His shirt and trousers soon joined her dress on the floor. "We'll have to make camp in the dark," he teased.

"Who cares?"

They embraced, framed in the window, awash in the vermillion radiance of the half-sun that peeked from between two lines of thunderclouds. Rebecca's lips met Carl's. Mobile and eager, they soon parted to admit his insistent tongue. A shiver of delight accompanied the pressure of his erect member against her lower belly. Their hands got to work, busily exploring familiar ground. Each touch, each caress, excited them more.

Rebecca moaned repeatedly by the time Carl lowered her to the floor. He had scraped their clothes together to form a crude pallet. Her knees elevated, Rebecca spread her legs to welcome him. Carl knelt, then bent forward. His kisses along the inner side of her thighs electrified her. Certain of no one near by, she squealed in delight as he reached the fevered mound at the junction.

Carl's hands went to her breasts, began to manipulate both nipples while his lips and tongue did lyrical things to her dewy cleft. Her heart pounded and the muscles of her abdomen contracted in regular waves, timed to each bold thrust of his lingual muscle between her fragrant portals. Bells rang and chimes shivered in her head. Carl grew more ardent in his ministrations and Rebecca felt her mind whirl in dizzy delight.

"Turn around," she pleaded. "Straddle me end for end." Quickly he did, then sucked in a stream of air between suddenly clenched teeth as she took him into her mouth. Her tongue described spirals on the broad tip of his pulsing phallus. Slowly she eased more of the silken shaft past her tugging lips. Carl remained on his knees and elbows, his whole body working with the power of their oral loving.

Waves of incandescent sensations engulfed them. Moment by moment the ultimate explosion grew closer. Rebecca's left hand found his pendant sack and began to knead it. Carl murmured his appreciation and gave more power to his slathering of her pleasure node. Rebecca keened around his massive prod.

Like a new dawn, rapturous completion burst first in Rebecca, then for Carl. They pulsed and shivered their way through a moment of oblivion and then sank in a heap to recover. Faintly, from far off, they heard the opening rumbles of the storm. It added a fitting climax to their happy event, Rebecca thought giddily. A large, magenta crescent remained a hand's breadth above the horizon.

"Oh, how wonderful," Rebecca observed. "We have time for more."

"I couldn't be happier," Carl told her lazily. "This is like a dream come true."

"You used to dream of making love with a woman in a playhouse in the trees?" Rebecca asked, ready for anything in her pleasant happy mood.

"Well, not exactly. I did want an arbor playhouse as a boy, I told you that. There was this big old tree

132

outside our house. I could see most of it from my bedroom window. I used to lay awake at night and look at it and imagine all sorts of adventures in the house of my desires. True, some of those imaginings led me into what the preachers call the 'secret vice.'

"But I never conceived of the idea of making love with a half-Sioux beauty like you in my hidden house," Carl went on, rising on one elbow. "All I can say is I'm glad it happened this way."

"You're sweet, Carl. I'm happy too. Now, before we lose the light, do you think . . . we might try something more conventional?"

"Of course," Carl eagerly acceded, stirring himself. "That storm looks to be moving this way. Do you think we should lead our horses over this way and spend the night here in the tree?"

"Lightning seeks the tallest object around," Rebecca reminded him.

Carl shuddered. "Then I suppose we spend the night in the rain and the mud."

"We have a tent, if you want to set it up and we have time to do so," Rebecca prompted.

"And what if that becomes the highest thing on the prairie?" Carl asked teasingly.

"Maybe we can stay in here after all. It's obvious the tree has never been struck by lightning in the past."

"Hummm. Well, we can decide on that later. Right now, I think I'm about to ravage you in proper nature loving style."

"I'll scream," Rebecca warned.

And she did. Carl entered her swiftly, buried his massive member to the hilt and then began a long grind-and-thrust coupling that sent shivers through them both. Rebecca clung to him and urged him on with words and inarticulate sounds. Bliss covered them, the storm changed direction and their loving went on long after the sun had disappeared for the day. Howling through multiple climaxes, Rebecca gave in to total abandon and enjoyed their unworldly tryst to the fullest. Only after they had become too drained to perform again did they dress and go for the horses.

Captain Grant Willis, U.S. Army, stood at the window of his office watching the unexpected arrival at Camp Cobb. His face took on a pained expression when he saw the gold fringed, blue regimental flag that denoted a field-grade officer. What the hell was an entire regiment doing there?

"Sergeant Tucker," he began as he turned away to address the company first sergeant. "Is there a special inspection or parade I don't know about?"

First Sergeant Casey Tucker frowned in concentration to search his memory. "No, sir. Not that I know of. Looks like we're in for some sort of visit from the bigwigs," he added with a nod to the window.

"Couldn't have picked a worse time. We've got details out riding the ravines for sign of Walks Proud and someone comes up with a brilliant idea like having an entire regiment pay us a visit."

"Best we get outside, sir."

"Right you are, Sergeant," Capt. Willis agreed as he fastened the top three buttons of his tunic.

By the time the captain reached the front porch of headquarters, the long column had been formed into companies on the parade ground and faced left, with the colors trooped behind two officers and the regimental sergeant major. Willis snapped off a crisp salute before he recognized the commanding colonel.

Short, squat, with a pinched face that seemed to register severe discomfort all the time, Col. Lydell Simms sat his bay horse looking every bit like a twelve year old got up for some pageant or spectacle. A long, straying tuft of his dark brown hair blew in the breeze and revealed a good deal more gray than the last time Willis had seen him. He returned the junior officer's salute with an indolent, almost insolent gesture. His pursed lips thinned out into a bloodless line.

"Well, Willis, it is expected custom for you to have been out here to greet me."

"Had I known you were coming, Colonel . . ." Willis started to defend himself until Simms cut him off.

"Didn't they teach you the 'No excuse, Sir,' answer at the Point, Willis? Or have they abandoned that since my day?"

Grant Willis had never liked the testy little martinet. He had, in fact, developed an instant dislike when they first met upon Willis' posting to Fort Sill. What particularly galled was the fact, discovered several months after he had been assigned to Camp Cobb, that Simms had never matriculated through the corps of professional officers, in effect, he had not attended the military academy at West Point, New York.

Simms was a "political officer," one of that crop who had bought his commission during the War of the Rebellion. Somehow he had managed to connive a way to retain it during the severe reductions after Appomattox. Why, hell, even that fair-haired hero, the Boy General, Custer, had been reverted to his rank of Lt. Colonel after the war. Yet, Lydell Simms had kissed the asses of enough politicians or someone in the War Department and retained a rank to which he should have never been promoted. Worse, he blatantly lied about his military background.

Willis had learned that from his first sergeant. Tucker had served under Simms in what the veteran noncom termed, "the worst regiment in the Army of the Potomac." Confiding in Grant Willis, as a first soldier has an unwritten right to do, Casey Tucker had labled Simms as arrogant, self-righteous, and, worst of all for a soldier, stupid.

"More'n once, he turned tail and ran just when we had the Johnny Rebs cryin' for mercy, Cap'n," Tucker had told him.

Now this ninny pulled a surprise visit. With a start, Grant Willis realized that Col. Simms had been talking to him for some while. ". . . naturally will retain your position as Post Commander, but . . ." Simms paused for effect. "But, command and control of all troops here will be mine."

Willis fought to keep his face from registering his shock and outrage. "I beg your pardon, sir, but that is contrary to the Standing Orders of the Army, sir."

Simms' beady, close set eyes narrowed. "You forget that I outrank you by three grades. This topic is not open for discussion." Instantly Simms raised a hand and brushed at his pencil-line mustache with his bent left index finger. It was a nervous habit he indulged constantly.

There had to be a way around this, Willis fumed, and he'd find it sooner or later. Meanwhile he did the only thing he could. "Very well, sir. Would you like to inspect *your* headquarters now, sir?" Willis relented.

Col. Simms produced the twisted grimace that served him for a smile. "That's quite satisfactory.

First I would like for myself and my staff to get shut of trail dust. While we do, you can empty your office and move to more suitable quarters."

Goddamn that arrogant bastard! If thoughts could kill, Grant Willis' instant attitude would have blown Lydell Simms clear off his horse. He had to bite the inside of one cheek before he could make a reply.

"That won't be necessary, sir. We have an office on the second floor of the headquarters for visiting dignitaries, usually generals, that should be perfect for you."

"I prefer to be on the ground floor. And there's no occasion for you to use that office either. You could set up in a corner of the orderly room."

"Sir! I am not a clerk. I must officially and formally protest such lack of consideration, sir. It demeans me in the eyes of the men."

Simms brushed his mustache again and pursed his lips. "Which is neither here nor there. You will attend to the daily operation of the post and leave the men to me."

"No, sir! This goes beyond inconsideration, beyond even rudeness. This is petty and vindictive and I'll speak up as I see fit on the subject. What you propose also violates Army regulations, to be specific, that portion dealing with the authority of a post commander. One of us will indeed use that office and we will—at least I will—conduct myself in front of the troops in a manner they will perceive as harmonious with you."

"One more word and I'll have you thrust in the stockade," Simms hissed icily.

"Do it and be damned," Capt. Willis snapped, beyond restraint.

"What's this? Insubordination to go along with willful failure to obey a lawful command? Very well, then. Captain Willis you are relieved of your command. You will confine yourself in your quarters and have no contact whatsoever with any member of this command, or with any officers, troops, messengers or couriers from Fort Sill. Do I make myself clear?"

Capt. Willis glared at the hateful face before him. "Quite clear, Colonel. Yes, indeed. And where am I to take my meals?"

"They will be brought to you, and be grateful I don't make it bread and water."

"As you say, sir," Capt. Willis grated out.

He snapped to the position of attention and rendered an elaborately dignified salute. Then he turned sharply and stalked away toward Officers' Row. The day would come, Grant Willis promised, when that son of a bitch got his.

Colonel Lydell Simms' arrival at Camp Cobb ruined the day for Walks Proud also. Four ranks of armed and painted warriors rode under their tribal and clan war chiefs, spread out over a quarter mile, headed east from the Washita toward Camp Cobb. Two outriders spurred back to the loose gathering of Indians and went directly to Walks Proud.

"Many hands of soldiers come to the soldier place," one explained excitedly. "More than one hand of soldiers for each of us to fight."

Walks Proud furrowed his brow and rubbed a hard palm against his chin. "We will stop here and I will ride forward to see this," he decided.

Together with his scouts, Walks Proud proceeded an hour's ride to the east, where they could observe Camp Cobb from a wash some six foot deep. They

hobbled their horses in a stand of black jack pine
and bellied forward nearly a mile in the gully. Close
enough then to clearly see the figures swarmed
around the army post, they watched intently.

"Too many," Walks Proud said at last. "We have
good medicine, but not against so many. These are
he bluecoats who hunt for me," he surmised cor-
rectly. "They will not stay together at this place for
long. When they leave, then we will attack as
planned. Any bluecoats who stay at this place will
lie."

13

Before the end of his first day confined to quarters, Capt. Grant Willis opened his door to three burly enlisted men who had come to move him and his possessions to another, smaller, cabin on Officers' Row. The colonel, he was told, would be occupying the larger, more comfortable accommodation of the post commander. Silently fuming, he complied. Now, three days later, he watched the arrival of an unusual pair.

Seated straight and tall, the man in whipcord trousers, loosely fitting shirt and vest, would qualify as handsome to any woman, Capt. Willis considered. Although the distance from the far end of Officers' Row and across the parade grounds prevented Willis from clearly making out the features, the man had a vague familiarity about him. His companion would be lovely in any costume. The Indian dress, Sioux, Willis judged, made her ravishing. Her long, raven locks, done in braids and secured by beaded strips of rawhide and some rabbit fur, bounced lightly on breasts that would take second to no other. Seated upon a big, spotted-rump Palouse horse, her dress had hiked up to reveal a tantalizing flash of leg.

He longed for the chance to speak with them, ally aware he hadn't a chance under the conditions f his confinement to quarters. Sighing, Capt. Willis turned away from the window and looked at the rumpled balls of paper that lay in a semicircle round the wastebasket. He chided himself for not eing able to marshal his thoughts well enough to rite a coherent report to Gen. Britton. He had to uash his anger to do so.

Willis took his place at the table and lifted a eel nib pen, fighting that anger. All he needed to o was lay down what happened, in a dispassionate anner and send it off to Headquarters. Tucker, is First Sergeant, would smuggle out the communication, of that he was sure. With powerful onging, he looked back at the strangers as they ode out of sight beyond the short street of lodgings.

Rebecca and Carl halted at the tie-rail in front of ie headquarters at Camp Cobb. Both had noted nd commented on the unusual construction of the utpost. A low, circular wall of black jack saplings, hardly higher than the head of a man seated n a fair-sized horse, enclosed a taller, square fortication made of native sandstone and larger logs. Vatchtowers at the four corners extended beyond ie palisades and gave clear fields of fire parallel to hem. All of the gates, they observed, stood wide pen. Sentries manned them, but gave only perunctory examination of visitors. They dismounted nd climbed the steps to the porch.

Carl surprised Rebecca by speaking the name of ie post commander to the sentry at the door. "We vould like to speak to Captain Willis."

A confused expression came to the young soldier's face. "Ah—er—maybe you better see the First Sergeant. Go right in."

First Sergeant Tucker greeted them and heard the request. His brow furrowed and he spoke softly. "The Captain's in his quarters, Mr. Blake. It's a bit irregular, but if you'd like, I can show you there."

"That's fine, Tucker. Lead on."

Surprised even more by this familiarity, Rebecca held her questions for later. She noted Carl's reaction by way of a raised eyebrow when they did not go to the large house that had a sign clearly identifying it as the post commander's residence. At a smaller cabin, Tucker knocked diffidently, and the door opened.

"Carl! By God, it's good to see you here," Capt. Willis greeted affably.

"Grant." To Rebecca he offered a brief explanation, "We knew each other back east at school. Grant, I want you to meet Rebecca Caldwell. Capt. Grant Willis."

Willis took Rebecca's hand and held it tightly. "Charmed. I saw you two ride in. From this distance I didn't recognize you. You've—ah—changed, Carl."

"A touch of fever in one of Panama's ranker swamps," Carl explained. "And the Sahara sun, no doubt. What are you doing here in the middle of the morning?"

Willis looked embarrassed. "I'm—ah—confined to quarters."

"By whose order?" Carl snapped.

"Colonel Lydell Simms. His regiment is out to round up a renegade named Walks Proud and his hostiles. He rode in here and just took over. No orders relieving me of command, nothing. Tucker's

142

since told me he did have orders to establish his own headquarters here, signed by Gen. Britton, but nothing that authorized the action he's taken." The words came in a rush, Willis relieved at having someone in whom he could confide.

"We know about Walks Proud," Carl replied. 'But if Simms is an independent command, by what authority does he relieve you and confine you to quarters?"

Willis formed a grim expression. "Out of spite, I suppose." He paused, shook his head as though to clear it. "I'm sorry, that sounds petty. We've never gotten along. He's a phony and I know it. Unfortunately, he knows I know it. Add to that the fact we disagree on just about everything; the military's role here, Indians, keeping whites out of the Nations. He saw his chance, thought he could get away with it, and took it." He shrugged.

"Not for long, I can promise you, Grant."

"You're a true friend, Carl. I appreciate anything you can do. Now, I asked what you were doing out this way and you never got around to telling me."

"We—ah—Becky here, Miss Rebecca, is quite an accomplished negotiator with the Indians. She's staved off several uprisings and knows the Army's limitations as to what can and can't be granted to the Indians. We've come to see what can be done about Walks Proud and his war."

Grant studied Rebecca closely, skepticism printed on his clear, tan features. Then he noted the pair of Colt Bisleys on her hips and the steady calm of her eyes. Quickly he revised his opinion. Lovely, true, but this one was a fighter.

"I've heard of a Rebecca Caldwell up in the Dakotas, shot the hell out of a gang of outlaws, was

143

it? Also made peace between the Arapahos and Shoshone out toward Yellowstone? I'd gauge you are one and the same."

"My fame, or perhaps infamy, precedes me, Captain Willis. Yes, and because of what I have achieved in past Indian disputes I believe I have a good chance in this one." She paused and gave Carl a wink. "Explaining all this to you is a good rehearsal for your area commander."

Willis smiled warmly for the first time since the indignity of his removal from command. "General Britton will give you a fair and unbiased hearing, I can assure you of that, Miss Rebecca."

They chatted easily for a while, took coffee with Willis and then decided it would be best to pay a call on Col. Simms. Willis held out little hope of a cordial reception. Simms made it often and loudly known how he felt about civilians mixing into what he considered strictly Army business.

Rebecca and Carl found that was indeed the case a moment after RSM Hans Grauber ushered them into the colonel's presence. "State your business and be brief about it," he snapped, not even waiting for introductions.

Carl and Rebecca stated their names. Then, succinctly as possible, Rebecca gave him an overview of her background and experience. Smiling to soften the presentation, she concluded with, "Carl has also had considerable experience with uprisings and tribal warfare. So, we felt it only proper for us to offer you our services as negotiators. I feel certain I can get most of the present agency-jumpers back where they belong and you can deal with the fanatical dissidents."

Col. Lydell Simms' haughty expression forecast

144

his words. "I regret that you have traveled so far for nothing. Negotiation is the farthest thing from my mind. *Extermination* is what my regiment will visit on these savages. You can't talk to mad dogs, you don't reason with them. You shoot them." He stopped abruptly and sized up Rebecca once more. Then he asked rhetorically, "So you're half-Sioux, are you?" At Rebecca's nod, he raised his voice. "Sergeant Major Grauber! In here, please."

Grauber banged open the door and slammed himself into a rigid posture, right arm bent in a salute. "Sir, yes, sir!"

"Sergeant Major, it seems," Col. Simms purred in velvety tones of self-congratulation, "that I have caught a half-breed, renegade spy."

"Now see here, Colonel," Carl began. A raised hand from Simms cut him off.

"Do you think I'm not aware that both of you visited a man under confinement? That alone is a violation sufficient to put you behind bars. We're under military law out here, and *I am the law!* If you would like to be incarcerated in the post stockade along with this spy, I'm sure I can accommodate you." To Grauber, "Summon the Provost Sergeant, Sergeant Major."

"Yes, sir."

Fire flickered in Carl's eyes. "This is preposterous, Colonel Simms. Rebecca Caldwell is a person well-known and respected in military circles. She's been invaluable in past cases of uprisings or inter-tribal warfare."

"She's not so highly regarded in the circles I travel in," Simms responded icily. "The offer's still open if you wish to see our stockade from the inside. Think about that."

145

Carl still had the wild glint in his eyes, yet he said nothing. Rebecca looked imploringly at him. He seemed to swell and prepare for an outburst, then he sighed heavily and turned on one heel. Disappointment and confusion registered on Rebecca's face as he strode through the door without a backward glance to reassure her.

Dust boiled up in the long, deep wash. Twenty-seven Apaches, led by *Intchi-dijin,* rode in to join the combined force outside Camp Cobb. Walks Proud greeted them warmly and embraced Black Wind in manly roughhouse. Stone Knife took the newcomers aside to point out the highlights of the hidden camp.

"It is good that you come," Walks Proud declared.

"It is by *Pa-nayo*'s own mischief that we found you," Black Wind responded. "We have been searching for a hand of days now, since we broke out of the bluecoats' cage at Fort Sill. You hide better than a raindrop in the desert."

Walks Proud laughed heartily and clapped him on the back. "We have to outwit your friend, Coyote. It is how we stay free. But we'll be seen, and soon, when we destroy this place the bluecoats call Camp Cobb."

"When will that be?" *Inchi-dijin* asked expectantly.

"Not long now, I would say. I have men watching the tall pole place. They report much activity through all of this day."

"I would like to go and see this for myself," *Ne-pot-on-je* injected.

146

"As I would do," Calico Turkey added.

"*Ugashe*—go," Black Wind commanded. "Bring back word of the soldiers."

Quickly they went, accompanied by two of Walks Proud's men. The Kiowa half-breed led his Apache ally to the center of the camp, to introduce him to the other sub-chiefs. They sat together and ate the midday meal, talked of what had been done since last they had feasted and danced to victory. Shortly into the afternoon, Bear Watcher and Calico Turkey came back, visibly excited. They hurried to Black Wind.

"They are going," *Ne-pot-on-je* blurted out. "The little soldier-chief with the big mouth is taking the bluecoats away from the fort."

"I would see this myself," Black Wind muttered.

"So would I, brother," Walks Proud declared. "It is something I have predicted and waited for a long while."

Led by Bear Watcher, the sub-chiefs accompanied Walks Proud to a vantage point where they could observe the fort. True to the young Apache's report, the regiment rode out in neat order, all bright and shiny. Each company, as it left behind the outer wall, turned to another point of the compass and set off at a fast trot. Obviously they intended to make a grand sweep to locate the hostiles. Walks Proud smiled as the patrols disappeared over the horizon.

"Bring up all the others," he spoke softly. "Now is the time."

Twilight spread a soft, soothing hand over the angular structures of Camp Cobb. Capt. Grant

Willis stood at his window again, gazing disconsolately across the parade grounds toward the headquarters building. Beyond that the open pairs of gates gave access to the rough terrain to the west. The outpost's design had been his own, he reflected.

Done as a classroom project at the Point, he had devised the double wall, square-within-a-circle battlements with a thought in mind of countering the Indian tactic of encircling an intended victim, be it a wagon train or a small village, and attacking constantly from all sides. It would work well, he believed, to foil the use of cavalry and siege engines in more orthodox fighting. He had received a 99 on the drawings and the model and not thought of it again.

At least not until his assignment to Indian Territory and the posting to Camp Cobb. Someone had seen his model and drawings and carried out in full size the unusual design. He later learned it was Lt. Gen. Albert Britton. The young—for a general—commander of Ft. Sill had even complimented Willis on the efficiency and ease of construction.

"Saw them at the academy one time and admired the concept. I'd have given you a hundred, but instructors at the Point aren't known for altruism," the General had remarked.

Now those walls confined him ever so surely as they repelled unwelcome company from outside. His confinement had not ended with the departure of Simms and his regiment. That left two rather green lieutenants in command.

Not good enough, he realized a minute later when unclearly defined figures ghosted through the lengthening shadows and scaled the outer wall, to

148

drop between it and the inner keep. Others, covered with dusty blankets, could be seen crawling toward the gates. It took Willis no time to recognize them as Indians. Confinement be damned, Willis snapped at himself as he started for the door.

Outside, he bellowed forcefully, "Sergeant of the Guard! There are hostiles between the walls! Sergeant Tucker, shut the gates, turn out the men."

Bugle notes floated through the twilight. Ahead of him, Big Belly saw the gates start to swing closed. With loud yips he urged his Kiowas forward. It's odd, he thought. He didn't see Walks Proud anywhere. Big Belly dismissed it and gained the forefront of his wave of warriors.

Swiftly the Cheyenne braves followed in a race for the gates. Pony Nose came abreast of Big Belly and gave him a friendly, challenging wave. "It's a good day to die, brother!"

"Then let the bluecoats do the dying," Big Belly shouted back.

Off to his left he saw the Comanches swarm toward the outer wall. Smoke appeared in a long curve of the defenses and three warriors fell from their ponies. Although he could not see them on the far side of the camp, Big Belly heard the Apaches engaging the troops as well. They had to make it through that gate. Lips set in a grim line, Big Belly lowered his lance and targeted a soldier struggling to drop a thick securing pin through a loop of iron and then into a hole in the ground.

The slim lance-point entered flesh and Big Belly gave it a cruel wrench to free the wedge of metal. Then he flashed on past the one closed gate. Beside him, Pony Nose hooted eerily and discharged his rifle toward the inner wall. Suddenly the inner gates slammed shut. The Indian force broke and divided, forced to circle between the battlements.

Now they took fire from both sides, though the exposed soldiers along the outer wall died quickly as more hostiles poured into the breach. From beyond the second palisade, Big Belly heard a loud, though calm, voice giving commands.

"Get that into place men, hurry. Load canister," Capt. Grant Willis ordered. "Get that saluting gun ready also. Load grape."

Dust and powder smoke blended in a thick haze that obscured the fight between the walls. Big Belly nearly rode down a Cheyenne brave who struggled on foot with a soldier who swung his empty rifle like a club. Urging his mount closer, Big Belly reached out and smacked the soldier on one cheek with the flat of his lance point. Yipping in delight, he turned to find another enemy.

All around him, Big Belly saw the wisdom and medicine of Walks Proud. It had been difficult to train warriors used to fighting from the back of a pony to construct long ropes of braided horsehide and work grease into them until strong and supple. The three-pointed hooks, like those the white men used to catch fish, fixed at one end puzzled Big Belly at first. Then Walks Proud explained they would be thrown over the walls and braves could walk up the steep palisades by pulling themselves along the ropes.

Now fully four hands of warriors did this, their heads already nearing the top of an undefended part of the inner wall. Halfway down, another four hands of men worked their way upward. There, the first lot had their shoulders over the top.

"To the left, over there," the same calm voice

shouted. Then, a moment later, as the warriors cleared the parapet, "Fire!"

Two deafening roars came in nearly the same instant that the twenty warriors got swept off the battlement by canister and grapeshot. Big Belly stared incredulously and began to wonder if they had made a terrible mistake.

14

Captain Grant Willis found himself in command of only the garrison complement and a platoon of troopers. His timely discovery of the attacking hostiles had partially secured the outer gates. Those of the inner wall had been hastily secured only seconds before the Indians dashed into the killing ground between. For the time being he had them where he wanted them.

He doubted that they knew that. They certainly didn't act like fish in a barrel. First Sergeant Tucker reported to him, eager for action and he sent the veteran Indian fighter to take charge of the inner wall defenses. Willis checked the spare loads for his revolver and set about rounding up the artillerymen who manned the field piece and saluting gun at the camp.

"You'll have to live with the recoil," he instructed them. "We need the limbers stored so we can quickly point anywhere needed. Load canister in that twelve pounder, grape in the six."

"Beggin' yer pardon, Cap'n, but if we use grape, we might hit some of our own," the sergeant in charge objected.

"Sergeant, if there are enough Indians to warrant

expending a round, none of ours will be alive in the impact area," Willis told him grimly.

More men climbed to the battlements and the volume of fire increased. Caught in interlocking fire, the hostiles suffered heavy losses. The Cheyenne warriors gained the top of the wall at one spot. Capt. Willis saw them and reacted swiftly.

"Over there, to the left." And as soon as the two cannons bore on the enemy, "Fire!"

Twenty Cheyennes flew backward off the wall. A sudden outbreak of firing and a number of dark heads rising above an undefended portion of the rear wall drew the captain's attention.

"Those are Apaches. Swing the guns around and give them a couple of rounds."

Here and there the hostiles had managed to ignite the black jack saplings that comprised the low outer wall. Flames licked to the sky. The Apaches kept coming and the two cannons grew hot from answering the threat. Once more, Pony Nose and his Cheyennes moved to a silent portion of wall and threw over their grapnels. Swiftly they climbed and dropped over onto the other side.

Pony Nose found himself in the camp stockade. Voices from the barred windows of a low building called to him in a number of Indian tongues. "Go," he commanded. "Get those people out. We must hurry."

Inside the building, the hostiles found twenty Cheyenne, Osage, Kiowa and Comanche prisoners. Some awaited military trial and execution, others would be doomed to banishment to a military prison in Florida. All wanted out. Gunshots and the scream of tortured metal filled the stone structure. Two guards burst through a door and died swiftly.

Freed prisoners began to stream out of the cells.

Among the other prisoners, Pony Nose saw a woman in a beaded doeskin dress and glossy black braids. He hurried there. "You are Dakota," he said in the Lakota tongue.

"Hecitu welo, Šahiela. Oglalak'hca, Tišayaota," Rebecca answered him over the din.

"The Red Top Lodge Oglala," Pony Nose repeated. "I know them. *Hiyu wo, micu,"* he called her forward, offering a hand and calling her sister.

Considerable headway had been made in tearing away parts of the inner bastion. Blocks of sandstone and several poles now lay in the space between it and the outer wall. Comanche braves worked industriously, their squat, muscular bodies ideally suited for the hard, heavy work. Slowly the breach grew. Someone got the idea to employ some of the grapnels and they were set in place, which cost the life of two warriors, then mounted men took the ropes and sprinted their ponies away.

Swiftly the ropes grew taut. They hummed like living things, then chunks of the wall burst outward. Uttering war whoops in high tremolos, the eager hostiles rushed inside. Quickly the breach filled behind them as more warriors, eager for white blood, hurtled through.

Suddenly the breach became a slaughterhouse. Capt. Willis and his gunners fired point-blank, one gun at a time at the howling enemy. They cut them down in swaths. Dead and wounded littered the parade grounds, though none reached the mid-point. Grapeshot and canister slashed at the Indians, who slowed, then stopped. Realization that every weapon in the camp had been turned on them created a mass panic.

Like a single man, they turned and scrambled for safety beyond the menacing mouths of the cannon.

They stumbled over their dead and only a few snatched at the upraised arm of a wounded comrade. In seconds the camp cleared of the enemy. From the wall came an excited shout.

"Cap'n; they're pullin' out. Turned tail."

Cheers broke out. Scowling, Capt. Willis mounted to the northwest blockhouse. Through a narrow firing slit he watched the bouncing rumps of Indian ponies dwindle. A thick layer of dust hung some ten feet off the ground. Somehow he had the awful premonition that they would be back.

Rebecca Caldwell found herself in the middle of a milling, jubilant camp of warriors from four nations. Pony Nose, who told her his name, kept her close by, a vigilant eye on the Apache and Comanche warriors aroused by blood lust. He assumed the air of a protective older brother, although hardly two years her senior.

"My little brother, Raven Heart, and I rode through the hoop of the Red Tops on our way to loot the dead at the big battle on the Greasy Grass," he told her while the Indian forces continued to mass.

"I was there," Rebecca said softly, a note of sorrow in her voice. "My father, Iron Calf, died in his lodge on the day of the fight."

An expression of awe crossed Pony Nose's face. "You are that *Sinaskawin?*"

"Yes. And my heart is heavy that our cousins the *Sahiela* fight with this wrong thinking mystic, Walks Proud. He is a half-breed, you know." She said no more, satisfied that the seed had been planted.

Pony Nose frowned. "This is a new thing to me. You are sure he is not of pure blood?"

155

"Yes. His name among the whites is Simon Black-thorne."

"Tell me more of this when . . . all of these have quieted down."

They sat beside a willow while the noise gradually diminished. Here and there along the wash, excited individuals recounted their deeds of bravery in the face of the white enemy. More sought food and clean, fresh water. A few more began to dismantle their small, squat lodges. At last, Rebecca risked a direct question.

"Will you ride away now that the fight is over?"

"Walks Proud says no. The fight is not over. We will bring our lodges down on the place of the white soldiers. There, out of range of their guns we will circle it and let none in or out."

"A siege," Rebecca said in English.

"Hokh!" Pony Nose blurted. "I forgot. It is said that the daughter of Iron Calf had a white mother."

"Hecitu welo," Rebecca admitted it.

"What were you doing in the white soldiers' iron house?" Pony Nose asked, suddenly suspicious.

Rebecca twisted her lush lips into a moue of distaste. "A soldier-chief put me there as a spy for Walks Proud."

Pony Nose chuckled appreciatively. "And now you join Walks Proud."

"Not . . . all together," Rebecca contradicted. "Like I said, my heart is heavy that you and my other cousins follow Walks Proud. It is bad for the Cheyenne, for the Kiowa, too. It is believed among some of the whites that Walks Proud has another purpose than the one he tells you."

"What would that be?" Pony Nose demanded.

"I—I don't know."

A camp herald started to cry out in a shrill voice,

156

repeated in the three major languages of those present, as he rode along the wash. "Down lodges. Pack up. We ride to the soldier place. There we will dance and feast and let them see us celebrate our victory. Walks Proud calls to all his brothers. Come snare the white soldiers like rabbits in a ring of the true people."

After only the briefest of waits, Brigade Sergeant Major Brandon Doyle admitted Carl Blake to the office of Lt. Gen. Albert Britton at Ft. Sill. The general rose, extending both hands. One to be shaken, the other to return a folded sheet of paper.

"Welcome, Mr. Blake. Your credentials are most impressive. The President speaks quite highly of your ability."

"Thank you, sir. I can only hope the President has not misplaced his trust. It seems I have already lost an important playing piece in this game against Walks Proud."

"What's that, Blake?" the general demanded.

"A young woman, sir. A delightfully lovely young woman at that. Rebecca Caldwell by name. She is also known as White Robe Woman of the Red Top Oglala. The President told me of her and suggested I try to make contact. She's quite formidable in dealing with hostile Indians."

"Hmmm. Yes, some fracas up on the high plains a year or so ago, right?"

"That's it, General. And at least a dozen times besides in which she has averted a general uprising by one tribe or another. I looked into it and discovered she was in route from Arizona Territory to Texas." Carl produced a fleeting smile and snipped the end from a fine Havana cigar. "I managed to cross paths

157

with her, introduced myself and we struck a bargain about this trip to look into Walks Proud."

"Rather a risky undertaking for a special agent of the President, don't you think?"

"Oh, Beck — ah — Rebecca's not aware I'm an agent. She sees me as a gentleman adventurer, sort of a black sheep third son of a wealthy Eastern family. World traveler, that sort of thing."

"You've come to know each other rather well, I gather?"

Carl developed a pink flush in spite of his effort to prevent it. "Ah — yes, one could say that."

"How is it, then, that you've come to lose this paragon of Indian negotiations?" Gen. Britton didn't intend for it to sound sarcastic.

"One of your officers as a matter of fact, General. A regimental commander named Simms. He's apparently taken over Camp Cobb and relieved the post commander there. He took it on himself also to arrest Rebecca as a spy for Walks Proud and chuck her in the stockade. He threatened me with the same treatment if I tried to prevent it."

"Lydell Simms." Gen. Britton said the name as though labeling the contents of a chamber pot. "He was to establish his own headquarters, to administer his regiment out of Cobb. He had absolutely no authority to usurp Willis."

"So Grant told me when I saw him there. That's what got your colonel riled enough to lock up Rebecca. Seems to me that this Colonel Simms is running around missing a few buttons."

"He's a hothead, a real fire breather when it comes to Indians. Wants to kill all the Indians on the reservations. I thought that if he knew himself at all it would give him some insight on what made Walks Proud run. Since we've finally reached that subject,

158

the President said in his personal letter to me that you would have some information on Walks Proud."

"Oh, yes, quite startling it is, too," Carl Blake assured the general. First of all, Blackthorne — Walks Proud — is secretly backed by some powerful influences in Washington and the New York banking community. Men who, for purposes of profit, want an Indian war to wipe out all the red men."

"The same old story of land speculation and railroads, I suppose," Gen. Britton speculated.

"There's more to it than that. Some of these men believe that there is oil, a whole lot of it, under this 'useless' land given to the Indians. The demand for kerosene, cleaning fluid and other products from petroleum is growing enormously. Fantastic fortunes can be made. Anyway, Blackthorne fits their plans perfectly. He hates his Indian side and is blind to any cause, save money. The President appointed me as a special Inspector General for him in his capacity as Commander-in-Chief of the Army. As such I'm empowered to take direct command of troops in the affected department. Naturally, that does not include superseding your command, General," Carl ended with a chuckle.

"I should hope not. But, why didn't you spring this on Lydell Slmms?"

"First off, Rebecca knows absolutely nothing about it. I didn't feel it was the time to reveal it to her. Also, I lacked a sufficiency of force to make it stick if I had followed.my instincts to relieve Simms and have him clapped in the guardhouse. When I return to Camp Cobb, I expect to be able to deal with Simms. Now, I have here," he went on as he reached into a coat pocket, "sealed orders for you from the President, regarding the prosecution of the Walks Proud campaign."

159

* * *

Pony Nose carried two bowls from the Cheyenne cookfires. One he gave to Rebecca. Already settled into place around the hapless army outpost, the ring of hostiles quite effectively sealed it off from outside relief. After releasing her bowl, Pony Nose swept an arm around the encampment.

"I have been thinking about what you say. And I've talked to some among the warriors who are, like me, husbands and fathers."

"I'm interested. What do they say?" Rebecca returned between bites of a savory stew, made lively with a lot of red peppers.

"Not all are in agreement with Walks Proud. Some say his medicine is failing. I know only too well that his claim to invincibility has been proven false. We have lost too many men."

"You are quite right, Pony Nose. Warriors died in the attack today and more will die in this siege. A wise man might suspect there is more behind Walks Proud's desire to stir up trouble with the whites than he implies."

"You speak wisely. Wet Owl, a Kiowa who is old enough to be my father, told me of meetings between Walks Proud and some shadowy figures who came and went from the sings and were never seen by anyone but Walks Proud. He also tells me that there will be such a meeting some time the night after this."

Rebecca stopped eating. "I think I would like to get a look at that meeting, maybe overhear what is discussed."

Pony Nose produced a sheepish grin. "So would I."

"Then we'll do it. Have Wet Owl send us word when Walks Proud leaves and what way he went."

160

* * *

Red-orange smudges glowed all around the besieged Camp Cobb. Drums throbbed and the survivors of the initial attack listened to the
singing—which First Sergeant Tucker described as
"caterwauling"—to celebrate the few scalps taken.
Mostly, the warriors danced and chanted to work up
courage for the next day's intended assaults. Capt.
Grant Willis and Sgt. Casey Tucker waited until well
after midnight.

"It's time, sir," Tucker whispered from close beside
the sally port gate.

"Right, Tucker. Well, Corporal Andrews, it's all on
you. Walk your horse around and through the open
outer gate. Troopers stationed there will be closing it
behind you so you've got to move out quickly. Don't
mount up until you're sure of having a run for it."

"Yes, sir. I'm ready."

"Good man. And, good luck, Andrews."

"You are fairly certain that Col. Simms will be
along Wildhorse Creek, sir?" Andrews asked.

"That's what Tucker heard from that Dutch Regimental Sergeant Major," Willis assured him.

"With luck I can be there before sunup, sir."

"Good. Find him and tell him how urgent it is."

"Will do, sir."

Andrews left, his bay troop horse at his side.
Hoofs muffled by rags, the sturdy cavalry mount
made little noise. At the main gate, the courier exchanged quiet words with three men from his company and faded out into the night.

He picked a spot where the Indian fires appeared
furthest apart and guided toward that place. Andrews had luck with him. The moon had not yet
risen. Ground plowed soft by unshod ponies aided in

suppressing noise of his progress. Out at what he estimated a thousand yards from the camp, he came upon the reason for no fires.

Andrews found himself in the fringe of a large pony herd. Several animals snorted curiously, only to quiet when his own beast returned a reply. He remained afoot, easing his way through the grazing horses. A questioning, albeit, young voice called out in a tongue he did not understand.

Instantly, Andrews halted and breathed softly through his mouth. The query was repeated, then silence. He waited for a long count of a hundred, then started off again. Gradually the Indian ponies thinned in number and he found himself on the far side of the herd.

"Good boy," he whispered into his mount's ear. "Only a little way more."

At what Andrews judged a quarter mile from the circular encampment, he stopped again. He bent and removed the rags, then swung into the saddle. A touch of the round knob cavalry spurs set the courier on his way.

Quickly oriented by the stars, Andrews set his course for Wildhorse Creek. He rode on through the night, guided by the late rising moon. Frequent intervals of walking to rest his mount improved, rather than hampered, his progress. Shortly before dawn he reached the small stream.

Daylight let him see the wide trail left by Col. Simms' headquarters, the battery of artillery, and the Gatling gun. They had pushed on west. Andrews followed and came upon the column at ten minutes of eleven that morning. He sought out Col. Simms at once.

"The damned gall of these savages," Simms erupted when Andrews finished his report. "This is n outrage. The audacity of these heathen Indians is unbearable. Worse, we've lost an important strategic asset in that camp."

"Beggin' your pardon, sir," Andrews injected. "But the camp is not taken as yet. It's under siege, but Capt. Willis has done remarkably well in organizing the defense and ejecting what hostiles breached the walls."

"Willis is it?" Simms asked nastily. "He's under confinement. I'll see to severe punishment for his breaking parole."

"If you please, sir, had he not done so, we'd all have been killed. He saw them first and gave the alarm. Now, sir, it's urgent, imperative, that your regiment ride to the relief of the survivors."

"By the time I could assemble the regiment and ride back there, it would be destroyed anyway," Simms muttered, more for his benefit than the messenger. "Attach yourself to the column, Corporal and we'll continue the search for Walks Proud."

"Colonel, sir, beggin' yer pardon, sir, but Walks Proud and every goddamned hostile for a hundred miles around is right outside Camp Cobb, sir," Andrews answered in spite of his concern over being insubordinate.

"I will take that under advisement, Corporal. Meanwhile, join the column and we'll proceed."

Twenty minutes later, when the headquarters company and artillery battery stopped for the noon meal, Cpl. Andrews slipped quietly away and walked a mile before mounting and streaking off westward toward Fort Sill.

15

"Come in and have a seat, General Blake," Lt. Gen. Britton boomed when the Brigade Sergeant Major's knock announced Carl's arrival. "As you see, I've had a chance to read the President's orders and a personal letter to me. He's made it clear that you will have the privileges of brigadier rank for this term as Inspector General, with right to supersede or relieve any officer you see fit, depending on the circumstances. He has also suggested I present you with the phrase, 'clam juice.' "

Carl chuckled. "That refers to clams on the half shell and my practice of sipping the juice from each individual shell, once I've finished the sweet morsels, rather than pour the contents into the cup provided and drink it off at the end. The President considers it a disgusting habit."

"So he says," Britton allowed, with a hurrumph. "Which also indicates I'm speaking with the right man. Very well. How much do you know about adulterous activities on the part of Colonel Lydell Simms?"

"Somewhat more than the President put in his communications to you. He felt it prudent not to reveal too much in writing. Simms has money, old

164

family money, of course. Yet recently he has been making rather large deposits from some source as yet unidentified by us. Most of that has been by direct deposit drafts on the Grace Bank in Manhattan. His attitude toward Indians is well-known and it is suspected that his influential friends in the War Department and at the Capitol arranged things for him to get this posting." Carl paused, drew a deep breath and sighed it out.

"Some of those same political cronies have also been depositing bank drafts from the Grace Bank. Interestingly enough, there is a dormant, though substantial account at the same bank, in the name of Simon Blackthorne."

Lt. Gen. Albert Britton's lips pursed and a cleft formed between his bristly brows. "I . . . see. Does the President suspect any direct connection between these obscure facts?"

"*Only* suspicions at this time, let me emphasize. Other agents are looking into that aspect. I have trouble adding a column of two figure numbers."

"Always the man of action, eh, Blake? Tell me, what was it like, graduating the Point and right away heading off to England and a four year course at Oxford?"

Carl produced an impish smile. "Fascinating, of course. And, considering I was actually in England to learn all I could about the British Army and any of the government's military ambitions for our War Department, an exciting assignment."

"General Sherman informs me that your involvements in England nearly got you in a fix."

"Nearly got my damned guts carved out. The Zulus. Remember, they compared Isandlwana with the Custer battle? I was there."

"Then by rights you *are* a brigadier."

"That's correct, Albert. Though I never wear a uniform."

"You're only a couple of years older than Custer when he wore a star."

"I've had my Little Bighorn, thank you," Carl chuckled. "Now, back to our immediate problem. No doubt the President emphasized to you as he did to me the importance of capturing Walks Proud alive for questioning if at all possible." Gen. Britton nodded. "If not, the absolute necessity of insuring his demise. I've no stomach for killing a man who has surrendered. But in Walks Proud's case, I doubt that will be a consideration."

"Nor do I," Britton assured him. "I have dispatch riders out to the regiments. We will depart tomorrow as scheduled and rendezvous with the rest at the Washita. Then on to round up Walks Proud. In the process, I feel certain we'll find opportunity to deal with Lydell Simms."

Carl showed a brief, grim smile. "I'm looking forward to it."

Late on her second night in the besiegers' camp, Rebecca Caldwell sat with Pony Nose while the drums throbbed and warriors weaved their intricate patterns of illustrative dances. The day's attacks against Camp Cobb had accomplished little or nothing. Judicious use of artillery had kept any large force from reaching the walls.

Those who did were driven off or trapped between the outer lunette and the inner battlements and destroyed. Unused to this sort of fighting, the young white squaw saw little purpose in wasting lives, yet Walks Proud kept hurling men against the fortifications with little concern for the results. In her quiet

166

eflection it occurred to her that in spite of his words Walks Proud sought to devastate his own forces. She uminated on that possibility when Wet Owl came o them.

"Walks Proud has left the hoop of the Kiowa and s not at the dance ground. I think he has gone to see he strangers."

"Which way did he head?" Pony Nose asked.

"To the Snow Wind."

Rebecca rose with Pony Nose and they set out to he north of the camp. They covered a quarter mile without encountering another person. Their mocca-sined feet moved silently over the ground, with only an infrequent sibilant rustle from tufts of dry grass. The ever present insects made more noise. A short distance farther they encountered an odd phenome-non.

Voices seemed to rise from the ground itself. A little careful investigation revealed a streambed where arching banks nearly formed a tunnel over the nar-row ribbon of water. Pony Nose dropped into the de-file and aided in lowering Rebecca to join him. Stealthfully they advanced. They soon encountered a sheltered area where frosty starlight made silhouettes of four human figures.

Rebecca worked her way closer until she could make out clear meaning of the voices that rumbled in a low mutter. By the not quite American or British meter, she identified Walks Proud. Given that small flaw, he still spoke English with total familiarity, re-vealing himself to not be the unsophisticated savage Col. Simms had dismissed him as being.

"I appreciate what you've been telling me, gentle-men," Walks Proud said. "But I must say, Senator Trudeau, that you took a considerable risk coming here."

167

U.S. Senator Dalton Trudeau? Connecticut's well-known Friend of the Red Man? Recognition of the name stood out vividly in Rebecca's mind. His words burned new impressions over those she had held for several years.

"Risky, but necessary," the New Englander's twang rang through his hushed tone. "Simon, you're simply not doing enough to insure an uprising that will guarantee the elimination of the cohesive tribes. These savages must be scattered and forever disorganized."

"Senator no one can want that more than I," Walks Proud responded. "So far, the Army's policy seems to be one of containment, rather than all out war. Can't the Senate do something about this?"

"Certainly not I," Trudeau protested. "I'm the Friend of the Red Man, remember? I can hardly introduce a bill to compel the army to exterminate my dear red friends, now can I? A political solution is simply out of the question at this time. Given the right climate at the Capitol . . ."

"Talk," Walks Proud spat. "Nothing but the same old nonsense."

"Now listen, Mr. Blackthorne, we bankers can hardly lay claim to land still considered as reservations for the banded together tribes."

An icy sensation tingled along Rebecca's spine as she recognized the voice of Nathan Benjamin. A sliver of rising moon provided enough light to verify his identity. What was he doing here, and why? She had little time to contemplate it as the senator spoke again.

"Simon, it's imperative that you get on with razing Camp Cobb and slaughtering all the inmates, then pursue your war against the whites. If you fail us, those nice payments into your secret bank account will stop."

"We're doing all we can. Your friend, Col. Simms, doesn't need an excuse to kill off Indians, so eventually your enormous profits off of the land are insured anyway. Give us some time. Between us, you'll have your war."

"You're sure of this?" Trudeau asked.

"So long as I get my share, I'll do my part," Walks Proud answered simply.

Stunned by Walks Proud's cynicism and the revelation that Col. Lydell Simms had some connection to an enormous conspiracy to strip the Indians of the pathetic little they presently possessed, Rebecca Caldwell crawled back to where Pony Nose waited. His grim expression alerted her.

"I hear quite well in the dark," he told her. "My English may not be good enough to speak, but I understand. Walks Proud is all you said and more. He is of a black heart. My Tall Ridge people will no longer fight for him."

His declaration lifted some of the dark gloom from Rebecca's thoughts. "That's a relief, Pony Nose," she told him in Lakota. "How will you go about refusing to fight?"

Pony Nose's brow wrinkled in serious thought. "I have not considered this as yet. We may just ride away tonight or in the morning. Still, some will not believe. You must help me make them understand."

"I will, gladly," Rebecca promised.

A flash of movement caught the attention of Nathan Benjamin. He stiffened and stared intently into the darkness. He had seen what appeared to be a woman's skirt. Yet this was a camp of warriors only. Who could it be? Their entire security depended upon secrecy. He reached out to touch Walks Proud's sleeve.

169

"Are there any women with your war party?" he asked with what casualness he could summon.

"No. Not since our last camp beyond the Washita. Why?"

"I think I just saw a woman's skirt. Someone, anyway, spying on us."

"Wait a minute. Pony Nose and his Cheyenne freed a Lakota woman in the first attack on Camp Cobb. I hear words that she speaks against the fighting. She could have followed me."

"Find out. And when you do," Benjamin added ominously, "silence her."

Everyone but the headquarters clerks, quartermaster sergeant, stable master and provost guards rode out of Fort Sill. The rest of the brigade artillery rumbled along with the supply and commissary wagons, complete with the other three Gatling gun sections. Carlton Blake rode in the vanguard with Lt. Gen. Albert Britton. The three widely spread regiments would receive orders some time during the day to rendezvous with the headquarters at the Wildhorse Creek ford of the Washita.

From there they would proceed eastward to Camp Cobb. Carl considered the move untimely, despite the urgency to come to Rebecca's aid. A southwesterly breeze in the morning had built to a powerful wind by noon. It sent billows of gritty dust into the air and whipped along wisps of grass and small twigs. At the midday halt for a meal of lukewarm beans and fried fatback, talk centered on the blustery weather. Carl brought it to the general's attention.

"Is this going to get any worse?" he asked.

"We can certainly hope not," Britton responded.

170

"If it does, we could be in trouble. The tolerances on those Gatling guns won't allow for much wind-driven sand in the actions. Walks Proud is estimated to have over two hundred warriors with him. Without artillery and the rapid-fire guns, we'd be at a disadvantage.

"Not that we couldn't defeat him," Britton went on, as he rose and put out his tin cup for more coffee. "Though at a considerably larger cost in lives. I want this to go quickly and be decisive, in a single battle if possible."

"I like your approach to combat, General," Carl remarked, eyes fixed on the distance, where dark clouds hung on the horizon.

"Regarding this storm, I'd like to put on as many miles as we can before it hits, if it does come this way." Britton raised his voice and called for the brigade adjutant. "Col. Trask, have the trumpeter sound Boots and Saddles."

"Yes, sir. The men are every bit as eager as you are to get moving."

"Let's hope they stay that way," Britton rumbled.

By two in the afternoon an orange-brown haze masked the sun. Swirling volumes of red earth rolled like balls across the plain. Visibility shortened to five hundred yards, then two hundred. Grim expressions appeared on the faces of many seasoned troopers. The wind had become a persistent howl. At quarter past the hour, the column halted and the order was given for the troops to cover their noses and mouths with bandannas, doing likewise for their horses' nostrils. Remounted they rode on.

Hardly three minutes passed before a gale force blow struck them like an invisible wall. In the blink of an eye, troopers found they could not see the man next to them in the files. Horses whinnied in distress.

Passed from mouth to mouth, the orders ran along the lines.

"Prepare to dismount . . . dis—mount. Remove blankets from saddle fastenings. Draw picket pins and secure your mounts. All troops to cover their horses' heads and their own with blankets. Turn away from the wind."

On raged the dust and sandstorm. Buffeted by the stupendous gusts, the men and animals involuntarily moved about. Under direction of their sergeants, the troopers rigged safety lines and held on against the howling tumult. Fine bits of sand bit Carl's skin and drew spots of blood, despite the face mask. All sense of time and direction fled.

Minutes became like days in hell. Then, far more suddenly than it started, the storm ended. A final fierce whiplash of wind, then an awful silence, as the tempest roared on northeast. Men coughed and muttered softly. The horses and mules made ample sounds of discomfort. Slowly the column resumed the motions of the living.

"Get out from under those," the sergeants bellowed. "Fix water for your mounts, then yourselves. Look lively."

"Attention to roll call!" BSM Doyle bellowed.

Each company first sergeant began the litany. "Ambrose!"

"Here!"

"Arthur!"

"Here, Sergeant."

"Blume," another first shirt shouted.

In minutes each was able to report. Brigade Sergeant Major Doyle turned smartly to the adjutant. "All present or accounted for, sir."

"Very good, Sergeant Major," Trask played out the ritual. He returned Doyle's salute and pivoted

172

in turn to report to Lt. Gen. Britton.

"I'm pleased. Men have wandered off in storms like that. I certainly hope our other columns escaped its fury. When the water detail is completed, prepare the men to mount."

"Yes, sir," Trask and Doyle echoed.

Lt. Gen. Britton turned to Carl Blake. "That storm alters things somewhat. I'm concerned about Col. Simms and his regiment. I'm certain it wouldn't displease you to ride forward and make contact with his command, Carl."

Grinning, Carl answered readily. "Not at all, General."

"Proceed, then. And take with you my specific orders for him as well as your own from the Commander-in-Chief."

"With pleasure," Carl replied lightly as he turned to mount.

Two Kiowa warriors came to the lodge of Pony Nose. They spoke directly to the young war chief, ignoring Rebecca Caldwell, although their purpose was to summon her to the presence of Walks Proud. When she reached the lodge, she found the war council assembled. Walks Proud looked at her with contempt, then began in an obtuse manner.

"What can you tell us of the inside of Camp Cobb?" When she indicated she did not understand his language, he asked in English, "Do you speak English?"

"Yes."

He repeated his question. Rebecca answered that she had not been there long, and only saw the inside of the stockade. Walks Proud's eyes narrowed and his face flushed with anger.

"I say you lie. You are a spy, planted by the Big Mouth Soldier-chief. You make me angry because you are a turncoat to your own people."

"I am not here to spy," Rebecca rebutted. "If that were so, I would have been here and long gone."

"No. You want to know my plans for the next attacks. That you'll not get, but you will die for seeking them."

Several voices of protest rose from among the council. "This cannot be," one older member stated as he stood. "Killing a woman is rare among my people, and yours as well, Walks Proud. We must discuss this, think over it."

"Long Flint is right," another adviser took up. "True a woman is sometimes killed because of a moment's anger or lust. But to deliberately execute one . . ." He left the charge hanging.

For half an hour the council wrangled over it. In disgust, Walks Proud at last dismissed them. Once they departed, with only a single guard in attendance, he rounded on Rebecca with a mask of fury, lips thinned in a grimace.

"I am sick of the opinions of others. There's a better way to handle this. You will answer my questions or suffer long and loudly. First, how much do you know about me?"

Rebecca remained silent.

"I dare not use torture," Walks Proud said to himself, rather than for her benefit. "That could turn the council against me. That doesn't say I can't use some persuasion."

With that he hunched one shoulder and swung a muscular arm. His backhand blow rocked Rebecca and left a red, stinging mark on one cheek. Straight up from his side, the open palm strike on the same spot set off alarms of pain. Hard knuckles crashed into her belly. Rebecca felt her strength ebbing.

Only her wits could save her, she realized. Her eyes sought some advantage to even the odds. Near where she stood she spied a pile of her possessions. On top, the double Lawrence belt rig with her Colt Bisleys. Walks Proud hit her again and she dropped to her knees.

In the same movement, she snatched up her sheath knife and one of the .44 revolvers. Twisting at the waist, she swiftly stabbed upward under the rib cage of the only warrior in the tipi with Walks Proud. He grunted and fell away from the red smeared blade. Right arm leading front again, she took a shot at Walks Proud.

It missed and Rebecca used the shock value time lag to cut her way out the back of the lodge. Shouts of consternation rang from in front of the tipi. Walks Proud cried out in Kiowa. Rebecca grabbed up her cartridge belt and started to run. Behind her she heard angry voices and several reports from rifles and revolvers. None of the slugs came her way and she realized that Pony Nose must have come to her aid with some of his Cheyenne. It gave her new energy.

In the confusion Rebecca managed to reach the pony herd. A quick examination revealed her Palouse stallion. She forced herself to calm down as she approached *Sila*. She spoke softly. Her spirits rose when she saw that the big steed had a hackamore fitted on his head. She took time to fasten the cartridge belt around her waist, then grabbed a handful of mane.

With one lithe movement she swung onto the whickering horse. Alarm spread through the circle of besiegers. After a quick look around, Rebecca set off bareback, with only the hackamore to guide *Sila*.

175

Bent low, she pounded her heels into his ribs until they cleared the herd and broke into a gallop.

Elation filled her as she set off to the west, her escape assured.

16

The first to pursue Rebecca Caldwell turned out to be Pony Nose's Cheyenne. They formed a sort of rear guard and obliterated her trail. After placing several long swales and some five miles between her precipitous flight and the enraged hostiles, the Cheyenne swung away to the north, after wiping out the diverging hoofprints of Rebecca's mount.

Oblivious to this, the warriors dispatched by Walks Proud continued on after the Cheyenne, who had deserted the cause. Rebecca slowed *Sila* to a less bone rattling trot and pressed on westward. An hour went by and she tensed suddenly when tiny, mounted figures appeared out of the heat wave distorted distance. Could they have circled around her?

She drew aside to find out, hidden in a thicket of mesquite and cactus. Inexorably the five riders drew nearer. Within fifteen minutes Rebecca could determine that they rode like white men, a bit of news that relieved her somewhat. These strangers could be outlaws. One way or the other held little appeal. A few minutes later she heaved a sigh of relief as she recognized the features of Carl Blake.

Rebecca rode out of the thicket and waved. "Hello, Carl. What are you doing here?"

Her relief and excitement could not be concealed from him. His own gratitude at finding her safe and free bloomed on his face. "Why, I was just out for a little ride. Looking for Col. Simms as a matter of fact. A little question to ask about how the hostiles came to be besieging Camp Cobb."

"You know about that?" Rebecca asked, eager for news.

"Yes. We came upon a Corporal Andrews early this morning. He brought the news. And I've been worried sick about what may have befallen you, my sweet."

"Col. Simms locked me up as an Indian, the hostiles thought me to be one, too. Even to the extent of accusing me of spying on them. Which I was in fact doing. With rather surprising results."

"Save that for later. I'm glad you're here with me now. First thing is to find Col. Simms."

"Oh, that's easy. Everyone in Walks Proud's siege camp knows where the Soldier-chief with the Loud Mouth is chasing shadows. I think I can lead you there easily."

The rest of the detachment, fifteen more men, came forward and the small column set off. Rebecca's directions proved unerring. They came upon Col. Simms' camp in mid-afternoon. Rebecca remained among the troopers while Carl and Sergeant Mayhew approached the testy little colonel.

"What the hell are you doing here?" Col. Simms snapped.

"Beggin' the Colonel's pardon, sir, but it would be wise if you were puttin' a 'sir' on the end of that," Mayhew said with great humor.

"Stop your blathering, Mayhew," Simms snarled.

"Perhaps you should read these," Carl offered his credentials. "You will see that I am Brigadier General Carlton Blake, by order of the President and Commander-in-Chief."

Lydell Simms paled. He swallowed with difficulty and spoke shakily. "I — I — er — beg the General's pardon, sir." He took the papers and read. His pallor turned to lividity. "Authority of the President, indeed! I am in command here and I will make the decisions."

"Not for long," Carl threatened ominously. "I can and will relieve you of command if you fail or refuse to follow the instructions of the President and General Britton explicitly."

Outraged, Col. Simms blustered on. "This is preposterous! Sergeant Major," he yelled at Hans Grauber. "Take this imposter into custody."

"Sergeant," Carl clipped off to Mayhew.

Mayhew did a smart about-face. "Detachment, prepare to draw carbines . . . Draw carbines." He turned back and saluted Carl.

"Colonel, we are in the midst of a hostile action. Your present willful disobedience of a lawful order places you in jeopardy of your life. You and your Sergeant Major will be long dead before one of your men can lay a hand on me. Is that clear?"

"Yes," Simms hissed.

"Yes, *sir*," Carl pressed. "Now, then, hear the purpose behind these orders. First, you must answer for imprisoning Rebecca Caldwell, who came to help, not to spy. Second, you must explain why, with an entire regiment, you managed to allow the hostiles to lay siege to Camp Cobb. Lastly, you must expound on your apparent reluctance to hit the Indian force in the rear."

"Is that all?" Simms asked acidly.

"No. The entire brigade is on its way. The rendezvous point, which I'm sure a dispatch rider informed

179

you of, is the Wildhorse Creek ford of the Washita. You are to head in that direction immediately. Before you do, there's one other matter that needs some light. Rebecca?"

Col. Simms paled. After hearing the messenger's report of the attack on Camp Cobb and release of Indian prisoners in the stockade, he presumed the meddlesome young woman had been killed by the hostiles. What could she possibly add to this?

Rebecca rode forward. A small smile played on her face, evidence she enjoyed her revelation. "While a guest in the hostile camp, I managed to overhear a conversation between Walks Proud and three white men. One of those men was Senator Dalton Trudeau, another Nathan Benjamin, the third Seymore Roth of New York. A scrap of that conversation, involving fomenting of another Indian war, referred to your friend, Col. Simms.' What might they have been speaking of?"

Simms caved in. His bluster fled, to be replaced by a horrid sense of betrayal and defeat. How could he have been used by two men he respected and believed to be friends? He had known Senator Trudeau and Seymore Roth socially in the East and they had corresponded frequently. Shaken, he admitted as much to Rebecca and Carl. Then he went on.

"Lately the Senator's letters have contained suggestions and some strongly prejudicial opinions about the Indians and them being as blight on the land. Since my own sentiments regarding the savages is well-known, I never considered some ulterior motive. When Walks Proud began his uprising, I looked at it as only doing what came naturally. My God, I—I'm devastated. General Blake, I'll do everything I can to mitigate this imbroglio, to make amends."

"General? Carl, you never told . . ."

"Another time, please, Rebecca. It's rather involved."

Momentary anger flashed through Rebecca. "Including using me, misrepresenting yourself to me?"

"We'll talk about it tonight, please. Right now we have an Indian campaign to fight," Carl cut her off.

Chastened by this revelation, Col. Simms spoke circumspectly. "By the General's leave, sir."

"Go on," Carl told him.

"Sergeant Major, assign dispatch riders to round up the patrols and set them on the most direct route to the Washita. We will leave for there at once."

Now that's more like it, Carl thought. Maybe Simms knew how to soldier after all.

Walks Proud stood on a knoll overlooking Camp Cobb, well out of range even for the artillery. He wore a feather bonnet and all the regalia of a warrior's ceremonial outfit. Walks Proud had whipped up the hostiles through the night and into morning. They drummed and sang and painted for war. Listening to his voice from the mound, clear and sharp in the quiet morning air, they cheered repeatedly, then rushed to positions for yet another attack.

Eagle wing-bone whistles shrilled. Warriors made ululating war cries. Behind Walks Proud, old men beat out the heartthrob tempo of a war dance. Walks Proud raised his feather decorated lance and turned as he rotated his wrist. With a mighty roar, the Indians surged toward Camp Cobb from every direction.

Today we will overwhelm them, Big Belly thought, mentally repeating Walks Proud's words.

His Kiowas rode loose in their war saddles, bows, rifles and lances ready. Painted faces bobbed in long lines, in both directions. Feathers, singly or in

181

groups, fluttered in the soft breeze. Warm rays came from the sun, though not hot enough to make fighting uncomfortable. A new, special excitement coursed through Big Belly's veins.

This would be the time. All whites would die. Then the mighty allied war party would ride on to strike again and again. At last no white face would be seen this side of the Father of Waters. What a glorious day to die!

Stone Knife kicked his pony's ribs. He burned with eagerness to wet his lance point with the blood of the whites. A quick glance left and right brought instant corrections.

"Keep up, hold back there, stay in line. Walks Proud says our strength lies in staying together, like the bluecoats, not in individual attacks to show our bravery."

They would have plenty of chances for that when the soldier village opened to them. Many coups, many scalps, many white-eyes to torture and hear their screams.

"Show your bravery by showing you can do what you are told. Stay in line."

"It feels funny to fight like this," Bright Shield complained at Stone Knife's side.

"Walks Proud says that is why the pony-soldiers win and we do not. They fight like this."

Both Comanches flinched involuntarily when they saw the big, white plume of smoke rise from the top of the distant wall. A moment later they heard the rippling shriek of the approaching shell, followed by the dull thud of the cannon discharging. Then the charge burst only a few yards in front of them.

Its crack and roar punished their ears and their ponies twitched nervously. A great gout of dirt spurted upward in the smoke. Undaunted, the huge circle of three files deep continued to close in on the camp. Another belch from the wall.

This time the shell screeched right in between the first and second ring. Seven horses screamed and went down. One man had his head torn off, another his chest ripped open. Eight more received wounds. The Comanches exchanged uncertain glances, yet pressed on.

Impossible to be ten places at once, Capt. Grant Willis thought to himself. His face registered calm, through a black grime of powder smudges and dust. For two hours now his men had successfully fought off the determined attack by the hostiles.

Barely in time had the troops on the inner wall discovered the Apache tactic. Half a dozen had gained the parapet by the time his artillerymen had humped one cannon around. Grapeshot wiped the warriors off the glacis and a concerted rush accounted for the six inside. The initial impetus blunted, the hostiles continued to circle the outer wall.

Arrows glided over the defenses and landed randomly inside. At best they produced three minor wounds. Sgt. Casey Tucker had brought Willis news of that as he sought to better position the cannons. Three more hours went by before enemy action slackened.

"Tucker," Capt. Willis barked when the firing ceased.

"Sir!"

"Get water to the men and have them fed in place. Also send runners with ammunition resupply."

"Right away, sir. Ah, Cap'n, how long can we hold out?" Tucker asked in a lowered voice.

Capt. Willis screwed his mouth into a rueful

pucker. "If we get another onslaught like the last—and we will—we'll be lucky to fight it to a standstill. Ammunition is dwindling. We have only seven charges of powder for the saluting gun and four for the twelve-pounder. There's no more grapeshot."

"Shit! Ah—pardon my language, sir." Tucker paused, and considered the situation for a moment. "I may have a solution to some of the problem, sir. Let me send some men to the stables, sir."

Understanding blossomed. "To the ferrier's to be precise?"

Sgt. Tucker grinned. "Yes, sir."

Twenty minutes later, the artillerymen began to load horseshoe nails, chunks of broken shoes and other jagged edged material into the cannons. Sgt. Tucker showed up with three troopers who pushed wheelbarrows. He seemed lighthearted for all their disadvantages.

"Found these in the magazine, sir. It's loose powder in kegs, no cartridges, but if these fellers paid attention to their training, they ought to be able to measure out what's needed."

Capt. Willis grinned. "You're a gem, Sergeant. Get busy with that right now, gunners."

"Yes, sir," one corporal gunner responded. "We'll need more water for sluicing the barrels, sir, to put out sparks. Not like a clean burning silk bag."

"See to it, then," Willis ordered abruptly, his ears probing an increase in background noise from outside the camp. "I think they've worked up to another try, First Sergeant. See that the men are alerted."

Minutes later the hostiles threw themselves at the walls. Most had sipped of the bitter brew Walks Proud promised would make them proof against soldier bullets, all had purified themselves for a renewed effort. They came in waves, mounted and on

184

foot. Rifles crackled from the battlements in a dwindling number.

When a group of five went silent at the same time, First Sergeant Tucker bellowed out, "Fix bayonets!"

Grapnels clattered against the palisade. Whooping and shouting, Comanche, Kiowa and Apaches swarmed up the tautened ropes. "Get men with axes up there," Tucker shouted. "Quartermaster personnel, cooks, everyone. Get up there and chop those damned things down."

"They're bunching up on the back wall, sir," a pale-faced young lieutenant informed Capt. Willis.

"Swing those guns around," Willis commanded. "Load them well."

Some twenty hostiles reached the top and swung over. They began to fire into the defenders to both sides, while more of their brothers appeared and put bare legs over the stone parapet. Unopposed, others crowded behind them.

"Fire! Load and fire! Keep firing."

Shrieking through the air, the irregular bits of metal and flat-sided horseshoe nails scythed across the top of the wall. Warriors began to scream and wail, horribly gashed by the flying shards. In the center of one deadly charge, four braves became shattered red pudding that clung to yellow-white skeletons. Three more met a similar fate in a segment of the circular pattern of the six-pounder salute gun.

"Load! Fire! Load faster damnit!" Willis ranted, his calm shattered for the first time.

Return fire began to take a toll on the hostiles. Warriors dropped between blasts from the cannons. With a hearty yell, a troop sergeant led a bayonet charge that destroyed the last resolve of the invaders. Thoroughly routed, they crowded together. Panic seized them as they realized they had no way out.

The hedge of wicked blades closed in.

Some chose to leap over the side. Others laid down their arms. A few fought defiantly. Most died screaming their hatred of whites as their blood ran from stab wounds. Capt. Willis looked numbly at the scarlet spray around the head of one Kiowa as a soldier butt-stroked his jaw.

Capt. Willis didn't feel the hammering of his heart until the last warrior fell. In the momentary silence he released a pent-up breath and staggered slightly as he turned a full circle to evaluate the state of his command.

"By God, we did it, Tucker," he said lamely.

"Yes, sir," Sgt. Tucker croaked hoarsely.

"I don't think—I don't think," Capt. Willis tried gruffly. He paused and accepted the dipper of water offered by his first sergeant. He ran his reddened eyes over the desolation and the troubling number of bluecoated bodies inside the compound.

"One more like that and we're done for, Tucker."

186

17

Nightfall brought a slight respite to the defenders
of Camp Cobb. War drums throbbed and the night
sky became a circle of huge, glowing bonfires. For
endless hours the singing went on. Perhaps more effective, Capt. Grant Willis thought, then the actual
attacks.

He studied the drawn, gaunt faces of his troops
and recorded the effect of the savage celebrations going on beyond the walls. Few soldiers slept. They ate,
drank water and coffee, and watched. Occasionally
one would rouse and go to the latrine to relieve himself. A few talked in low tones. Mostly about home
and family. Several, Willis noted, prayed. He would
like to himself.

Regretfully, he doubted that he could carry it off
with the dignity of a George Washington. More
likely, he reasoned, the troops would think he had
lost all other hope and abandoned them to God's
mercy. Some time after midnight, with the volume of
the hostiles' celebration reduced by half, Capt. Willis
managed to get some sleep.

With the coming of dawn, the Indians returned.
Their numbers had been starkly reduced, yet they
advanced in full force. Obedient to signals given by

their leaders, they assaulted the walls from three sides at once. Willis bit his lip and withheld the vital artillery. Men battled with what they had. Most had been reduced to their sidearms.

Smith and Wesson Scoffield .45s popped along the battlement. Indians and soldiers alike screamed and died. The sickly stench of blood in inhuman abundance cloyed Capt. Willis' nostrils. Slowly all sounds of resistance ended from the outer palisade. Black hair and colorful feathers began to appear along the inner parapet.

"West wall, stand by," Capt. Willis commanded the gunners. "Ready . . . Fire! Load . . . Fire! Load . . . Fire! Load . . ."

"Beggin' your pardon, Captain," one gun captain interrupted the litany of commands. "This is our last round."

Shaken, Capt. Willis looked back at the cannons. The six-pound saluting gun sat idle. Its gunner had spoken only at the last minute. Willis swallowed. "Take your personal arms and go to the walls, then. The south, I think."

"Captain, we've got three rounds left," the gunner of the field piece informed him.

"Very well. Fire them there at the west wall, then fire the six-pounder. After that, join the others on the south wall."

"Yes, sir."

The end had come. Grant Willis knew it only too well. God damn that arrogant bastard, Lydell Simms, he prayed silently as he waited his fate, .45 Scoffield ready in one hand, a sabre in the other.

In the midst of their imminent victory, cries of

alarm came from the besiegers outside Camp Cobb. Their shouts had been taken up from those of others beyond in the circle of Indian encampments. A loud rumble preceded the sudden appearance of many Indian ponies.

With a wild sweep across the battlefield, the crazed animals ran down everything in their path. Behind them, lodges burst into blossoms of fire, the flames reaching toward the sky. More crackling blazes signified stacks of supplies going to the torch. Gunshots crackled and a bugle sounded the charge.

Like a suddenly ebbing tide, the red flow slithered back over the walls and sped off across the plain. Carbines crackling, the troops of Lydell Simms' regiment came into view. At once cheering broke out along the walls.

"By God, look at 'em run!" one veteran shouted.

"Pour it on 'em, boys," another weary, wounded trooper urged.

"Open the gates—open the gates!" Capt. Grant Willis shouted.

Half the regiment split off to pursue the Indians, while the rest streamed into the badly damaged camp. With them came Rebecca Caldwell and Carl Blake. When they halted before Capt. Willis, it became obvious an old argument had been resumed.

"Believe me, Colonel, it's the smartest thing to do. Reinforce the garrison and take the rest back out. Hunt down the hostiles," Rebecca urged, her points clipped off precisely.

"She's right," Carl took up. "Remember, I can make it an order."

Capt. Willis gave Carl a confused look at that remark. "You've come in time, sir," he addressed to Col. Simms. "I assume I'm to return

189

to confinement, now the siege has been lifted?"

Simms produced a sour expression. "If I could have my way, you would. With additional char—" He swallowed hard and shot a cautious glance at Carl Blake. "The disposition of your case is now up to this gentleman."

"Carl? What do you have to do with it?" Capt. Willis asked uncertainly.

"Brigadier General Carlton Blake, if you please, Captain," Col. Simms managed to get in his final modicum of spite.

"For God's sake," Willis blurted. "That's terrific, Carl—ah—General. When did all this happen?"

"Three months ago, in Washington. Special appointment by the President."

"Congratulations, Ca—General. But—well—if that's so, why didn't you tell me when—when you first came here?"

"Orders. Sorry, Grant. My specific orders were to report to no one except Lt. General Britton. Once the area commander knew, I was free to exercise my authority."

"What about—ah—Miss Rebecca here?" Grant stumbled.

"Officially she's in the pay of the Army as a translator and negotiator. Fact is, I couldn't keep her from coming along, short of locking her in the stockade at Ft. Sill."

"I see. But my larger concern was that the Indians broke her out of here after you left. I figured Miss Rebecca for dead or long gone by now."

"We liberated Becky and added her to the staff."

"Women in the military," Col. Simms sniffed. "That sort of unorthodox shenanigans won't do your career any good."

190

"Frankly, Simms, I don't really give a damn. After this campaign is over, my commission goes back on the shelf until needed again and I head for South America," Carl told him in an offhand manner.

Loud rumbles from wagons entering the compound interrupted further speech for a while. When they drew up on the parade grounds, Carl spoke to Grant.

"Let's see to getting the reinforcements positioned. Without the full regiment in pursuit, I have a feeling the hostiles might return some time tomorrow."

"Is there ammunition in those wagons?" Capt. Willis asked hopefully.

"Plenty of it," a major on Simms' staff informed him.

"First Sergeant, see that it is distributed. Now, with the Colonel's permission, I would like to have my men relieved. We've been under nearly constant attack or harassment for two days and nights."

"Do as you see fit," Col. Simms snapped bitterly.

"Come, man, put a good face on it," Carl asserted. "You still command your regiment . . . for now," he added sardonically. "It's up to you to follow the protocols."

White-lipped, Simms answered tightly, "Quite right, General." He drew a deep breath and rose to his full, insignificant height in the saddle. "Captain, it will be my pleasure to see that your men receive some well deserved rest. My troops can man the walls."

While the soldiers went about their martial tasks, Rebecca and Carl led their horses to the stable and left them in the hands of an attendant. A worry frown creased Rebecca's brow.

"Carl, I still don't like it. Even if Walks Proud's

191

hostiles are on the run, they could turn tail in an instant. If that happens, then we, too, are trapped inside here, with no certainty when the brigade will arrive."

"You are," Carl admitted, "only too right."

Walks Proud had seen the approaching troops of Col. Simms' regiment first and given the alarm. He had signaled for the retreat and organized the scattering of the warriors. All had gone according to a predetermined plan. Minimal casualties resulted. Walks Proud credited his superior white education to this.

Having learned to read and write, he could avail himself of any type of information. He chose military affairs, politics and the financial world as his specialties. He did well in two of them. Others took care of his investments, the secret bank accounts, and all the economic cares to insure a bountiful future, once the final Indian war reached the desired results.

To do that, he had to survive, Walks Proud kept reminding himself as he streaked toward the new rally point. There, at White Star Mound, he would rally his followers for one more, overwhelming attack. He had something there, promised him by Nathan Benjamin and his white friends, that would definitely turn the tide.

It would take the better part of a day, perhaps two, to instruct men unfamiliar with any form of technical device, how to prepare, load and fire the little French-made, rifled howitzer and to safely make deadly explosive packages out of scrap metal and sticks of dynamite. Once he

192

grew confident of the ability of his warriors to handle the deadly tools, they would attack again.

After being left to deal with his regiment as he saw fit, and more importantly, not being relieved of command, Col. Lydell Simms allowed his earlier attitude to drain away. He actually exhibited genuine concern for the wounded and saw that the medical officer attached to the regiment tended all who had need. He declined dinner with Carl and Grant and set up in the upstairs office at headquarters, thus denying it to a superior, Gen. Carl Blake.

At least, Carl decided as he talked about this with Rebecca, "Lydell Simms doesn't practice at being mean spirited, self-centered and nasty. He comes by it as second nature."

Rebecca laughed lightly. "Since I know you like I do, I have to believe that you're serious about that."

"I am. Simms got himself into something he hadn't the intelligence to properly evaluate. Probably didn't bother trying because he feels the same about Indians as those who will profit from such a war. The rest he acquired to insulate himself and his inadequacies from the professional military. Put together it makes him a prize . . ."

"Asshole," Rebecca completed for him. She started away from the porch overhang of the cabin on Officers' Row she had been assigned. Carl followed. "The stars are lovely tonight, aren't they? Hard to believe that a large force of hostile Indians is out there, still capable of doing a lot of harm to this place and to us."

"Don't think about them," Carl urged.

"What should I think about?" Rebecca teased.

193

Carl took her in his arms. Their lips blended in a long, soul satisfying kiss. "How about us?" he inquired when they parted.

"Us and what?" Rebecca advanced the word play.

Carl slid a hand in the arm hole of her Sioux dress and cupped a pert breast. "Do you have something in mind?" he cooed.

Rebecca reached downward and worked fingers between them. She closed on the rising bulk of his manhood. "Ummmm. It's a secret. Wild horses couldn't drag it from me."

Thumb on her nipple, Carl furthered the tease. "Don't be too sure of that."

"I think . . . I think we had better go inside," Rebecca suggested in short gasps.

"Fine idea. And then what?" Carl coaxed.

"I will show you something I know you'll like a whole lot."

"I like it already," Carl answered eagerly. "Will it take a long time?"

"If we're careful, it should last all night," Rebecca promised.

True to her word, with a wild tumult of emotions lifting them over and over to newer heights of euphoria, it managed to last until the first, pale, gray-white of dawn.

To everyone's consternation, morning brought another attack. Always scornful of the idea of a dynamic leader who could unite the tribes to fight more along the lines of civilized warfare, Col. Lydell Simms found it necessary to revise his belief. Whatever this Walks Proud was doing, it worked.

In spite of being outnumbered better than three to

194

one, the hostiles threw themselves at the walls with all the determination of the previous day. They employed a new tactic, which brought nearly fifty warriors in to the base of the outer wall under cover of darkness. That portion of the regiment which manned the battlements had been lulled by long, uneventful hours. Before they realized it, strong, silent braves scaled the palisade and dropped among them.

They fought silently, swiftly subduing those nearest the outer gates. Several dropped down and flung open the tall wooden portals. Other Indians swarmed in, none on horseback. Quickly they breasted the inner wall and again opened the gates. With wild whoops, horsemen galloped directly into the compound. Sleep drugged troopers spilled from their tents and barracks, to be cut down by arrows and bullets. Belatedly the alarm was given.

"They're inside," Capt. Willis bellowed. "Inside. Man those guns."

"My God, Captain, what happened?" a severely disconcerted Col. Simms demanded as he rushed up with his shirttail still out of his trousers.

"Somehow they got inside and opened the gates. The troops on the wall must have been asleep."

"I'll have every one of them court-martialed," Simms growled.

"If any of them live and if you do," Willis snapped back, fisting his service revolver.

Rudely pulled from their sweet lovemaking, Rebecca Caldwell and Carl Blake dressed hurriedly. They came from the cabin with weapons ready. Hand-to-hand fighting had broken out on the parade grounds. Everywhere they looked, Indians on horseback or afoot clashed with the soldiers. At such close quarters it seemed impossible to fire without hitting friendly troops.

"How did they manage it?" Rebecca asked.

"Someone slipped up," Carl said shortly.

"Whatever the case," Rebecca began, then paused to snap a quick shot at a mounted Kiowa. "We're in a lot of trouble."

Her target fell from his pony and lay still, shot through the head. Another took his place and rode toward the pair, lance lowered and ready. Carl's bullet missed by a hair's width, and the warrior closed with grim purpose. Rebecca's right hand Bisley spat fire and lead. The slug sent up a shower of bone chips when it struck a hair-pipe chest ornament, then smashed through the Indian's breastbone. His lance fell at Carl's feet.

"Close," Carl panted.

"Any closer and we'll be in the Spirit World," Rebecca replied darkly.

"I want to try for the gates," Carl suggested. "If we shut them in here they'll be cut off from the rest. Greater numbers will take care of it from there."

"Good idea. I'll cover you."

With a sharp bang, one of the cannons went off. A deluge of refuse shrieked through the air and slashed into fresh hostiles at the gate. Horses screamed and doubled up, pitching their riders head-first. Less than half the dozen braves raised up, most of them showing minor wounds. Rebecca turned toward the rear wall in time to see more Indians, Apaches by their clothing, pouring over the parapet.

Swiftly she ran to where Capt. Willis directed the limited fire of the big guns. She pointed urgently. "The back wall. Apaches coming over."

"Shift that six-pounder," Willis reacted instantly. "Give them a load."

Dust and powder smoke obscured the parade. Above it the bare flag pole made a mute witness. Dawnlight dyed the buildings pink. Rebecca sought some inspiration to rally the troops.

"Where's the flag kept?" she asked.

Willis blinked. Who cared at a time like this? "In the orderly room at headquarters. Shelf behind the First Sergeant's desk. Why?"

"You'll see," Rebecca promised. She brought Carl along with a jerk of her head.

A howling warrior darted to cut them off, only to stop in mid-stride and fall on his face, his heart burst by a .44 bullet from Rebecca's Bisley. With Carl covering her, she bounded up the steps and inside. Quickly she retrieved the banner and hurried from the building.

"Come on," she snapped out.

Carl came. Together they reached the base of the flagpole. Made clumsy by hurry, Rebecca unfolded the triangle of blue and revealed the edge of the red and white stripes. Carl shot a Comanche only five feet from them. Carl's slug shattered the warrior's bow before snuffing out his life.

Her fingers stiffened by danger, Rebecca fumbled the keepers into the metal grommets and pulled on the halyard. The cloth unfolded as it rose and snapped in a sunrise breeze. Several men noticed it and raised a feeble cheer.

More joined them. With a shout of bravado, twenty soldiers rushed from the barracks, bayonets on their rifles. Here and there the hostiles howled in rage and increased the fury of their assault. Men roused to fight them off, only to be forced back. Rebecca emptied one Bisley and drew the other.

She had fired two rounds and then realized that

197

more than half of the men had not seen the flag raised. Surely they would rally if they knew, she surmised. She needed something to draw their attention.

Music was the answer. There was a bugle call that went with raising the flag, Rebecca knew, but not the one she was hearing now. Crisp and clean, over the tumult of the battle, she heard the brazen notes of the *Charge*.

18

A moment later, a steady pat-pat-pat hammering f .45-70 cartridges announced the inclusion of a ‚atling gun in the battle. Two more opened up sec-nds later. Trapped between the double walls, with 1e brigade blocking their sole escape, the hostiles ould only flee into the compound. More troops oured after them.

"It's the brigade," Capt. Willis shouted.

"With the rest of my regiment," Col. Simms added 1 a sour tone. "We nearly got ourselves trapped in ere. Damnit, woman, I hate to admit it, but you 'ere right," he told Rebecca.

Given the respite, Rebecca Caldwell reloaded her :volvers. In confused panic, the Indians dashed round the camp. Some found a small sally port and ung it open. It forced them to depart afoot and 'ave behind their horses. Outside, Big Belly and 4ack Wind tried to rally the demoralized warriors. Vith a wave of his feathered lance, Stone Knife urst through the troops and brought out a dozen omanches.

Swiftly he organized the routed force and they ruck the left flank of the brigade. Men and ani-1als churned up dust and whirled about one another like leaves in an October gale. Inside, a nagging fact surfaced for Rebecca.

"Did you notice something? Walks Proud was not among those inside the compound."

"So what?" Carl asked during the brief lull in the fighting.

"We have to find him. Pony Nose is not far off. He and his Cheyennes will gather the council members and we need Walks Proud to confront with what we know of his scheme."

"It would be better to wait until the fighting is over," Carl suggested.

"By then it could be too late. I've noticed before that he never leads, only directs the fighting. He could escape. Especially now that the brigade has arrived. I don't see him as the martyr type."

"Good point. Only how do we manage this?"

"Get our horses and go after him," Rebecca stated simply.

Where had the other soldiers come from? Black Wind looked about at the carnage done by the long-shoot guns. Hardly a man of his Rise from the Grass People had escaped a wound. Several warriors had their bellies slashed open and sat glassy eyed with shock, slowly sliding into death. Those who were still able had joined Stone Knife in attacking the long column of soldiers. He had remained to drag injured men from the heat of battle. Regrettably, that's all he could do for them.

Protected by the glacis of the outer wall, they had shade and water. It would have to do for now. He sought a loose horse to carry him into the fight. Why had he listened to the Kiowa half-breed? He had led his brothers into a death trap. From the far side of the two walls' stronghold, he heard the steady rhythm of the shoots-fast guns. Men had to stop to reload. Not this terrible weapon. He didn't understand how it worked. Black Wind only knew that it shot faster than a line of bluecoat soldiers and kept on shooting.

Now the crump of artillery joined the pattering of the Gatling guns. A riderless pony trotted toward him and Black Wind stood. Waving one hand to catch the animal's attention, he reached for the braided reins with the other. He snagged it and soon set himself astride the broad back.

"I will be back for you, brothers," Black Wind promised as he jabbed heels into the nervous creature's ribs.

"They are too many for us to fight," Big Belly told his second in command.

"First we have to get out of here," Two Bows replied.

Big Belly grunted. "Then that is what we will do. Gather the warriors and we will rush the bluecoats in that opening."

In less than three minutes the word had been spread. Led by the Kiowas, the mixed band of Indians rushed around the camp one more time, then hurled themselves at the blocking force in the outer gateway. Caught completely by surprise, the troops got bowled over by the foremost ponies. Those behind them had no opportunity to fire on the hostiles.

Once clear of the deadly ground between fortifications, Big Belly set off at a fast pace toward the predetermined rally point at White Star Mound. He brought some forty warriors with him. Under attack from the left, the brigade could not detach men to pursue.

"It worked," Two Bows cried, laughing.

"Not until we are out of range, old friend," Big Belly yelled back.

"That won't be long," Two Bows observed. "Where is Walks Proud?"

"Gone ahead of us. We will see him at White Star Mound."

Rebecca Caldwell looked at the dwindling resistance. "We have to go now," she insisted.

"I—can't allow that, Miss Caldwell," Col. Simms rejected her proposal.

"It's too dangerous," Capt. Willis added.

Rebecca appealed to Carl with a glance. "I'm going to have to pull rank on you gentlemen," Carl began. "It's against my better judgement. Yet, Rebecca has a valid point. She got the Cheyenne to defect and they're out there somewhere. With them behind us we can compel the council to listen to the truth about Walks Proud. That will end the uprising without a question. We'll take along a small detachment to provide security."

"A company," Capt. Willis offered.

"Ten men, no more," Rebecca answered him. "We'll be at the stable."

"It is going well," Walks Proud reported to Nathan Benjamin when he reached White Star Mound. "The entire brigade is engaged now."

"But won't your losses turn the Indians from further fighting?" the "shyster turned banker" asked.

"There will be enough who survive to go among the people and foment another uprising, never fear, Mr. Benjamin. The red man does not trust the soldiers. Too often they have lied, misled and betrayed. Enough of that. Tell your associates it is going according to plan. Now you must leave before the survivors start arriving."

"Yes. That would be prudent. Which — which way should it be safe to go?"

"North and east. Head for the main trail that leads to Fort Smith, in Arkansas."

"Uh — well — ah, some past indiscretions make it unwise for me to show my face there," Benjamin stammered.

Walks Proud smiled without humor. "From the bad old days as a bunco steerer? Oh, I know about you, Mr. Benjamin. You came rather late to banking, didn't you? Bought your way in with the proceeds of a — ah, how do you put it? — big score?"

"Well, I wanted to change my ways. Make a new start."

"You mean you wanted to fleece people legally, rather than take risks with the law." Walks Proud made a forceful gesture, arm extended. "Go north then, into Kansas. But you must go."

"Yes — I — yes." Benjamin started for his horse. "Where can we contact you in the future?"

"A message left here will reach me," Walks Proud said stiffly.

"Very well. And good luck."

"You amuse me, Mr. Benjamin," Walks Proud stated after the banker rode off.

* * *

203

Dust still hung in the air beyond the ridge to the west of Camp Cobb. Rebecca Caldwell reined in *Sila,* the signal for the others to halt. For a long moment she studied the terrain between them and the horizon.

"Do we trail them all?" Sgt. Mayhew asked her.

"No. We'll go after that larger group of Kiowas. It's certain they'll know where to meet up with Walks Proud," Rebecca informed him.

"They swung a bit north of the rest," Mayhew said thoughtfully.

"Any ideas, Sergeant?" Carl asked.

"Could be a couple of places," the NCO responded. "That big wash where they had their camp on the Washita for one. Or maybe Butler Knob, what the Indians call White Star Mound. Then there's a low valley where Rush Creek joins the Washita, lots of grass even this time of year."

"We'll follow along for a while and see if you can pick it for us later," Rebecca suggested.

Two hours later, the detail stopped to rest the horses. Rebecca squatted and studied the divots left by unshod ponies. Carl and Mayhew joined her.

"They're pushing their horses hard," Rebecca observed. "And look there. Bloodspots. No telling how many wounded they have along."

"Any chance of our running into them?" Carl asked.

"Not the way they're moving. Well, Sergeant Mayhew, what place would you pick now?"

"Butler Knob," Sgt. Mayhew stated firmly.

Rebecca considered this a moment. "I think it's time to send a man back with that information and have troops brought up."

"At least a regiment," Carl suggested.

"They'll have to travel lightly," Rebecca added. "We want them in place at the right time."

"I'll see to it," Mayhew offered.

"We'll keep going. I want to find Walks Proud before nightfall," Rebecca declared firmly.

Suddenly Comanches sprang from the ground like new grass. Rebecca and Carl led the way over a rolling swale and down toward a meandering creek. Halfway there, the Indians rose out of the grass and began firing. Sgt. Mayhew yelled for a halt, the troopers drew their Springfield carbines and opened up.

More Comanches, on horseback, rushed toward them. Well disciplined fire forced them to swing wide and begin to circle. Their companions advanced on hands and knees, hidden by the grass.

"There must be thirty of them," Carl declared, his voice tight.

"Make it five less than they started with," Rebecca answered, the walnut stock of her Winchester against her cheek. The rifle cracked. "Make it six."

Eleven guns against the aroused Comanches seemed risky odds, yet the accuracy of their shots kept the Indians at bay. The ring broke, swung away, then reformed to make a direct charge. Those on the ground came from the opposite direction.

"Granger, Jones, watch those heathens," Sgt. Mayhew commanded. "Rest of you boys, knock them riders down."

Two volleys slowed the charge. A third cleared four Comanches from their mounts. Granger and Jones poured steady fire from their Springfields into the running warriors, dumping three before the leader realized he was taking hits. At once he yodelled a command and the Comanches dropped from sight.

"We can't take much of this," Mayhew said to Carl. "I know that. One more man wouldn't have made any difference. What we need is a convincer."

"We could sing," Rebecca suggested.

"Hunh! What good would that do?" Sgt. Mayhew rejected.

"Becky's got good instincts," Carl defended. "During the Zulu war, the Welsh boys of the Twenty-fourth Foot at Rorke's Drift confounded the wooly buggers by singing the regimental song," Carl countered. "It's worth a try."

"Well, boy-o, I hope it does the trick. Private Mastek, your a fairly good tenor. What say, you give us a bit of song?"

Mastek blinked, swallowed and gave a short nod. "Right you are, Sergeant. 'Let Baccus' sons be not dismayed,' " he began in a high, clear tone.

" 'Come join with me each jovial blade,' " two more picked up. " 'To sing and dance and lend me aid . . .' "

" 'And help me with the chorus," Mayhew's bass boomed out.

"They're coming again," Carl warned.

Each soldier's volume increased as they opened fire, their shots punctuated the words of the song. " 'Instead of spa we'll drink strong ale; And pay the reckoning on the nail; No man for debt will go to jail; From Garry Owen in glory!' "

Those words and the syncopated gunfire slowed the charging riders. They turned to left and right and began to circle again. In the midst of the mounted braves, Rebecca located a large, barrel chested warrior with full regalia done in tones of brown and black. He wore the bison-horn headdress of an important man. She recognized him as Big Belly, whom Pony Nose had identified for her. Taking a breath and expelling half, she sighted on his chest.

Her Winchester bucked and spat a .44 round in the direction of Big Belly. He reared in the saddle and slumped sideways. His pony carried him away from the circling Indians for a few long strides, then slowed to a standstill. With enfeebled arms, Big Belly tried to raise his aged Spencer.

Rebecca fired again. All strength left Big Belly, along with his life, as he fell from his pony to lie spread-eagled in the grass. Hoots of consternation and shouted words informed the Comanches their leader had fallen.

"You got their chief!" Sgt. Mayhew shouted to Rebecca.

"Not a chief, Sergeant, he was their war leader," Rebecca corrected.

"Whatever. They'll not be goin' on now."

"I wouldn't guarantee that," Rebecca offered glumly.

To verify Mayhew's words, the Comanches pulled back, taking the body of Big Belly, and disappeared with all the swiftness of their initial attack. Rebecca stood at Carl's side and watched them go.

"They're headed the same place we are," she stated.

"I'm afraid so," Carl agreed. "And now Walks Proud will know we're on the way."

With overlapping trails to follow, Rebecca and Carl led the detail at a fast trot. By four that afternoon, a low bell-shaped prominence could be made out on the northwestern horizon. Sgt. Mayhew called for a halt.

"Butler's Knob," he identified it, arm outflung to point.

"I suggest we find a place to keep out of sight until reinforcements come up," Carl put in.

"I don't like it, but I agree," Rebecca said, anxious to bring on a conclusion to the uprising. "After dark I want to go in close and scout the area."

"But, that's . . ." Carl began, then shook his head ruefully. "It won't do any good telling you no. We'll both go."

Mayhew sent a trooper forward who located a suitable wash. When the detail gathered there, Mayhew looked around. "Cold camp tonight. Can't risk a fire being seen over yonder on that knob."

It wasn't the first time Rebecca Caldwell had spent a night without hot food or coffee. She made do along with the others. After twilight dwindled into full darkness she and Carl started off for White Star Mound. By that time, large, winking yellow spots could be seen around the top of the knob.

"We should be able to get quite close. The chances are there will be a lot of drumming and singing, even some mourning rites for Big Belly," Rebecca opined.

"The idea is not to get caught," Carl reminded her facetiously.

"First thing on my mind," Rebecca advised him in like mood.

From there, they progressed in silence. They covered the five miles with relative ease. Crickets and katydids kept the night lively. Mosquitos rose in clouds from the creek and made a humming, whining hell through which they had to ride. By ten-thirty they had reached the base of Butler's Knob without encountering an Indian. Drums throbbed and singers chanted above them.

"They'll all be up top," Rebecca whispered to Carl. "Do we go there?"

"We do."

"I hope what we find out is worth the risk."

"We won't know until we do it, will we?" Rebecca jibed.

Halfway up Rebecca nearly stepped on the small of the back of a not-too-vigilant picket. A solid whack with the barrel of her Bisley put him into a deeper sleep than the one she had disturbed.

"Tie him up and put a gag in his mouth," she requested of Carl. "Then we'll go on."

Through most of the night, Rebecca and Carl observed the large Indian camp. From different positions they were able to estimate the number of warriors present. Also a figure on horses. Much to her surprise, Rebecca first discovered that women and children abounded in the big village atop White Star Mound.

They must have been slipping away from the agencies for more than a week, she estimated. If Walks Proud's uprising brought about a general Indian war, the braves would not want their families in the hands of the whites. Their presence posed both a problem and a possible tactical advantage. Rebecca stored all her impressions for later discussion and went on watching.

"Time to go," Carl suggested a few minutes after three in the morning. "They're all asleep now, except the honor guard, or whatever you call it, for Big Belly."

"Right," Rebecca agreed. "We have a lot to tell whoever comes up with the troops."

"Not all of it pleasant. It looks like for every brave killed at Camp Cobb, there's one or maybe more to

209

take his place right here."

"A successful war leader draws followers like flies to an outhouse. Give me a hand, will you?" Rebecca requested. "My legs have gotten stiff."

As quietly as they came, Rebecca and Carl slipped away into the night. Under a half-moon, they rode back to the hidden camp in under three-quarters of an hour. All they had to do now was wait for the Army.

19

Sgt. Mayhew sent two men to intercept whatever
relief column came from Camp Cobb to their aid.
They had instructions to direct the troops to make
the approach from the west, hidden by an escarpment at the base of Butler Knob that dropped off to
the banks of the Washita, some ten miles in that direction. Under cover of the last darkness, Rebecca
and Carl, along with Mayhew and his seven troopers, moved forward into position at the south base of
the mound.

Hidden by a small stand of Osage Orange trees,
they waited for the eventual sound of a bugle that
would signal the attack. Two hours after sunrise it
finally came. Against the disadvantage of attacking
uphill, the soldiers charged the knob and began to
climb.

"Here we go," Carl observed, with a nod to the
west.

Two platoons had detached themselves from the
general line of approach and swung around Butler
Knob toward their position. No doubt, Rebecca reck-
oned, the same would be happening on the other end
of the formation. That way, at least, the enemy
could be trapped on the top.

"We'll go up with them," she announced as she put a foot in *Sila*'s stirrup.

Confusion broke out in the camp that everyone considered to be safe. Women and children ran shrieking, horses bolted in the herd that grazed the south side of the knob. Warriors ran to catch their favorite war mounts. So far they had made no headway toward resistance.

"There are bluecoats everywhere," Stone Knife shouted to his Comanches. "Get on the horses. Make ready to ride."

"No!" Walks Proud's voice boomed from a rocky promontory. "Stand and fight. We can defeat them."

"There are too many," several voices took up protest.

"Are you old women?" Walks Proud taunted. Uneasiness gripped him. He could see his control over these warriors fading.

"What about the women?" Bear Watcher, the Apache, demanded. "And our children."

"Up here," Walks Proud commanded. "Bring them to these rocks. There is a cave. They will be safe there."

It gave them something to do, a sense of purpose. Walks Proud continued to call and gesture until the frightened women and youngsters started to straggle up the rise toward him. Then he gave orders for the defense.

"Fight from behind the rocks. When the soldiers get close enough, we will roll stones down on them. There is also this," he added, patting the large parfleche bags that held fused sticks of dynamite. "Get the horses and be ready to mount and charge the white soldiers."

212

"Will that drive them off?" Lame Deer of the Comanche asked.

"Yes," Walks Proud told him. "And we will win the day. Though many may die."

Several lodges had been taken down by their occupants. Walks Proud hurried from his vantage point long enough to countermand that activity. "Stop taking down lodges. Leave them. It makes it harder for the soldiers to see us if they are up."

From partway down the west slope the crackle of gunfire reached Walks Proud. A querying glance to Bear Watcher gave him an answer.

"Black Wind has taken his Apaches down to delay the soldiers."

They numbered only three hands of warriors now, enough Black Wind thought to break up the charge of the *pen-dic-olye* and make time to fight back. He had seen the bluecoats coming and gathered his remaining braves. He left Bear Watcher to tend to the women and children. How he missed *Wano-boono*. Brave as any three men, poor Calico Turkey lay with the other dead at the soldier camp. Many bluecoats would pay for that.

With the legendary skill of the Apaches, the small force worked through low brush until they reached a sort of shelf halfway down the knob. Under Black Wind's direction they spread out and lay in wait. The thunder of many hoofs could be clearly heard. When the right moment came, *Intchi-Dijin* gave the coyote howl signal.

Half of his men rose with blankets and flipped the loose ends in the faces of the cavalry mounts. The other half opened fire with rifles. Horses reared and whinnied in alarm. Men cursed and several fell from their saddles. Troops who had never fought Apaches

213

floundered in confusion and the charge blunted to scattered forays. Then, swiftly as they had risen from the ground, the Apaches disappeared.

Sergeants bellowed at their men to reorganize the line and advance. Slowly the disorganized mass became a cohesive unit and the files closed. Once again the cavalry started uphill. They covered twenty yards with ease, then the Apaches burst up out of the brush right in their faces.

More shots claimed victims and several riderless horses galloped away in panic. Before the troopers could recover, Black Wind sent his braves back to ground and they faded out of sight. Doubly cautious, the troops calmed their mounts and reformed for the charge. Certain they could not be surprised again, they urged the animals to a trot. With less than two hundred yards remaining to the top, the Apaches sprang out of hiding again.

This time they appeared behind the double line of soldiers. Firing a ragged volley, they popped out of sight and changed position. A coyote yip brought them up and they blasted at the demoralized soldiers. Then down again.

"Damnit, that's enough," a red faced captain shouted. "We've got them shut off from the rest. Turn back and cut them down."

"No, keep the line," his battalion commander demanded.

Too late. The troop wheeled and made for where the Apaches had last been seen. They received blanket fringes in their faces for the effort. Bullets cut the air and smacked into flesh. A horse and rider went down together, both shot through the heart. By the time the first soldier fired a shot, the Apaches had disappeared again.

214

Black Wind's delaying tactics paid a dividend. Walks Proud managed to reorganize his forces and they now poured heavy fire down into the ranks of troopers. Forced to withdraw, the cavalry rode from White Star Mound.

"They're falling back," Sgt. Mayhew declared in a tone of disbelief.

"Not on this side," Rebecca announced. "I say we keep going."

"Good enough," Carl agreed.

By then the blue uniformed troops had ridden up breast of them. A seasoned first lieutenant acnowledged them with a jaunty finger to his kepi and they proceeded up the hill. Slightly beyond the halfway point they observed that the Indians had their attention on the west slope, where the Apaches till harassed the retreating troopers.

"They don't know we're coming," Rebecca called cheerily to Carl.

"If the lads on the other side are keepin' up with us, we'll catch them all unawares," Sgt. Mayhew speculated.

His anticipation of events proved right as the half company reached the summit into the bowl-like depression that formed the top of White Star Mound. Surprised warriors scattered before them and at the officer's command, everyone held fire until they clearly saw more blue shell jackets beyond the cluster of lodges.

"Open fire!" the lieutenant commanded. "Targets of opportunity."

With only the delay necessary for sound to travel across the vale and back, the other troops responded

215

in kind. Caught between forces, it became the Indians' turn to panic. No sooner had they turned to do battle with the mounted menace than the routed troops on the west slope started upward again.

"Where did these soldiers come from?" a worried Kiowa asked Walks Proud.

"They got around us. Our Apache brothers fought only part of their number. There are many more than I expected."

"We're trapped up here," another Kiowa complained.

"Then fight harder," Walks Proud instructed sharply. "Take these, light them and throw."

More of the bundles of dynamite and broken bits of cast-iron pots passed among the defenders. Here and there men lighted cigars taken on raids or snatched brands from the morning cookfires. They lighted fuses and hurled them at the soldiers.

Blasts began to go off and again stalled the attack from the west. From north and south of the camp the enemy poured in unhampered. Soldiers pounded over the ground and in among the lodges. One paused to fire point-blank into a brush *wickiup*. Muzzle blast ignited the dry foliage and the dwelling roared up in flames. Sparks set off a neighbor, which in turn contributed to the conflagration. A bundle of dynamite sticks landed near the trooper and went off with a tremendous roar.

Ripped by the blast, he and his horse sailed some ten feet in the air and landed with a sodden thud. Thick, acrid smoke blended with that from the burning lodges and the weapons being fired. Through the confusion, Rebecca identified Stone Knife and brought up her Bisley.

Bucking with recoil, the big revolver rode in her

216

hand. Her slug gouged flesh from the Comanche's left shoulder and he dropped to one knee. His rifle came up and he sighted on Carl Blake, thinking him to be his attacker. Stone Knife's finger tightened on the trigger when Carl jinked his horse to one side, unaware of the danger he had faced. Rebecca fired again and the bullet took Stone Knife in the chest.

Swiftly she turned to confront a screaming warrior who ran at her with a lance. Her third round took him in the chest, high on the right. He dropped his spear and abruptly sat on the ground, a stunned look on his face. Here and there she noticed Indians with their hands in the air. More soldiers poured into the concave dish at the summit. Explosions tortured the ears of everyone. Driven back to the top, the Apaches joined the melee. In the wild whirl of battle *Intchi-Dijin* thought he saw an Indian woman fighting with the white-eyes. The smoke and dust cleared a moment and he recognized the woman who had escaped from the big camp. *She* brought the soldiers here.

Raging at this obvious betrayal, Black Wind shoved his way through the press of horses and warriors, past men struggling with soldiers, intent on revenge. His fury took voice and he screamed taunting insults at her.

Rebecca heard the angry sounds in an unfamiliar language and turned to see an Apache aim his rifle at her. She dropped from *Sila*'s saddle to the ground and fired wildly. His bullet cracked overhead and her horse moved out of the way. With a clearer field of fire, Rebecca pumped two bullets from the Bisley into Black Wind as he ran toward her, firing his rifle.

He staggered, stopped and turned sideways, then

217

fell face first in the blood-soaked soil. Gradually the sounds of conflict diminished.

"Carl, do you see anything of Walks Proud?" Rebecca asked with concern.

"No. Not that I'd know him if I saw him."

"He has to be here somewhere," she judged. "Let's leave the fighting to the Army and look around."

A five minute search revealed no sign of the renegade leader. By then the overwhelming force of soldiers had subdued the hostiles. Herded together they presented a dismal lot, faces solemn in defeat. Col. Farmington, who commanded the reinforced regiment in this operation, came forward.

Through interpreters he asked, "Where is Walks Proud?" He received no answer.

Rebecca and Carl continued to search. In the quiet following combat, a faint voice of a child came to her ears. She paused, looked around, puzzled.

"Did you hear that? A small child crying."

"Are you sure, Becky?" Carl asked.

"Positive. It seemed to come from up in those rocks."

Near the center of the meadow rose a jumble of boulders. Rebecca headed there. Her Bisley at the ready, she worked through the rocks always alert for any unpleasant surprises. A dark spot between two leaning slabs drew her attention and she approached with increased care.

"Carl, come here. It looks like some sort of opening that leads underground."

"Hold on," he warned. "We'd better get a lantern or some sort of light before going in there."

"All right. I'll watch it while you go for something," she suggested.

Carl started off a moment before a shouted alarm

came from near the rim of the basin. "More Indians coming in," a soldier called.

Rebecca left her vigil spot to yell advice to Col. Farmington. "Don't shoot. It might be the Cheyenne with the council of elders. Pony Nose and his men are not hostiles."

"Gen. Britton said nothing of this," Farmington countered her as he strode over to where she stood.

"I know. Pony Nose found out about Walks Proud and pulled his warriors out of the fight at Camp Cobb," Rebecca explained. "He sent for the council of elders of each tribe involved. He wants to help make peace."

"If I could believe that . . ."

"You can, Colonel. Believe me. Oh, yes, it is the Cheyenne. See, Colonel?"

"Ummm. They have a lot of gray-heads with them, too. This might be an odd place for a peace council, but I'm willing to try."

"Fine," Rebecca praised. "Now all we have to do is find Walks Proud."

Trapped among women and babes and stripling youths too young to fight; in the hushed babble of voices, Walks Proud paced a small portion of the cavern floor. Some quirk of nature had formed this pocket in the earth and so designed it that no second opening existed. It would be discovered sooner or later, Walks Proud realized. If only he had some way of slipping away before then.

His thoughts continued to plague him while the battle ended. With the silence outside came the recognition that his magnificent scheme had ended in disaster. How could he let himself be cornered like this? There had to be some way. Voices speaking English startled him as they came from the entrance.

"This is what I wanted to look into," a woman's words echoed.

"Watch your step now," a man urged. Then a pause as light streamed into the small cave, followed by a gasp. "It's the women and children."

"Yes. They must be terrified," Rebecca Caldwell stated.

Walks Proud glared his hatred at her, recognizing the woman from his encounter in the camp at the Washita. Slowly, so as not to draw their attention, Walks Proud raised his revolver and took aim at her head. At least she would not live to enjoy the victory.

Rebecca stiffened, then swung to her left, Bisley cutting toward her attacker's position. The hammer fell and flame gouted from the muzzle. She shot Walks Proud once, in the left leg. Impact and the pain sent his own round wild. It flattened on the rock slabs above and howled through the cavern. Now two guns covered him and his shoulders sagged in resignation.

Walking Bear of the Kiowa rose from his sitting place and placed a hand on the pipe in a gesture of asking for the floor. "We have heard all that you have said. It puts sorrow in our hearts, also anger. If what you say is all true, we have been betrayed by a brother who has pretended to have our best interests at heart."

Gen. Britton's interpreter, who had come up with the general and the headquarters company, translated the words. To Walking Bear's address, he

220

added, "They never were for this war, General."

"I know that," Britton sighed out. "Nor should they be punished for it. Tell Walking Bear that."

The Kiowa words flowed like heavy liquid. Walking Bear nodded and turned to address his fellow councilmen. "We would not be telling true things to say we like living as we do now. But it is better than fighting and dying for nothing, betrayed by one of our own. I say we turn this false Kiowa over to the Army. I say let him be hanged I have spoken."

Plenty Rains rose. "I am Comanche and I know no fear. Yet I would not have the numberless whites slaughtering every red man so some of them could get rich. I believe what they say. I, too, say let the Army have the traitor."

Agreement flickered around the circle. Several abstained from speech making, yet called for a vote. Carl exchanged a glance with Lt. Gen. Britton and Rebecca while the voting sticks came out of each man's possibles bag. Each of the elders handled his voting stick reverently, impressed by the power they represented.

Light Foot of the Cheyenne described the rules. "Black side up we leave this place and try to find a way to free Walks Proud. Red side up is yes, and we let the Army take him."

Several silent minutes went by. Then the elders began to put down their sticks, covered by their palms, until the last one had been placed before its owner. Light Foot nodded.

Hands moved away from sticks. Three black sides showed. All the rest were red. "It is done," Light Foot said softly.

"He'll hang, that's for certain," Rebecca told Carl

as they left the large brush arbor where the meeting had taken place.

"And that's a good enough end for him. Yet I want a chance to question him closely and for a long time before that happens."

"Then you'll be going after the men behind Walks Proud?"

"Most likely," Carl answered shortly.

"Would you want some company?" Rebecca offered.

"Are you seriously offering to come with me?" Carl asked, though he could not keep the hope out of his voice.

"I am. I got to thinking. If this is as big as you say, with so much at stake, I wouldn't be surprised to discover that Chris Starret is involved in some aspect of it. It might be we could solve two problems at the same time."

"I — Becky — I'm delighted. Even if we only solve one problem, having you along will make it all worth the while."

"Right now I have another problem to deal with," Rebecca moaned.

"What's that?"

"I want to get away from here, take a long, hot bath, and get in bed."

"Alone?" Carl asked, eyes twinkling.

"Not if there's any chance of you being around to help me," Rebecca cheered him by saying.

BOLT

An Adult Western Series by Cort Martin